J. WASHINGTON

That One Time My Mother-in-Law Kidnapped My Husband

First published by Dope Kontent Entertainment 2023

Copyright © 2023 by J. Washington

All rights reserved. No part of this publication may be reproduced, stored or transmitted in any form or by any means, electronic, mechanical, photocopying, recording, scanning, or otherwise without written permission from the publisher. It is illegal to copy this book, post it to a website, or distribute it by any other means without permission.

This novel is entirely a work of fiction. The names, characters and incidents portrayed in it are the work of the author's imagination. Any resemblance to actual persons, living or dead, events or localities is entirely coincidental.

#ButIfYouKnowYouKnow

First edition

ISBN: 979-8-9879018-6-1

This book was professionally typeset on Reedsy. Find out more at reedsy.com

"Why think separately of this life than the next, when one is born from the last? Time is always too short for those who need it; but for those who love, it lasts forever."

Contents

1. PROLOGUE: Love at First Sight — 1
2. The Diagnosis — 4
3. The Proposal — 25
4. A Dose of Reality — 51
5. Home Sweet Home — 75
6. So Close — 92
7. I-35 Road Warrior — 104
8. Shot Through the Heart — 121
9. The Black Door — 143
10. When Everything's Made to be Broken — 155
11. Tear-Stained Letters — 167
12. Let It Be — 177

Epilogue — 221
Chapter 1: New Orleans — 227
About the Author — 236
Also by J. Washington — 237

One

PROLOGUE: Love at First Sight

Her dad pulled up to their new home in his black, Cadillac Sedan Deville and parked in the driveway. Tanyah had been a little sad to leave all of her friends up north, in Massachusetts, but she was excited about the fresh adventure awaiting her. Plus, her main friends, who were really like her brother and sister, were moving down to Texas too since their dad and hers were in the military together; and that's all that mattered. Tanyah and her little sister, Renee, got out of the car and ran towards the front door, eager to see the inside of their first real house.

It was a one-story, light brown, bricked house with a large front yard. It seemed like every fifth or sixth house on the street was pretty much the same, except for the brick color or garage door placement. Tanyah was already planning on where to put her slip-and-slide since she'd heard it was always hot in Texas. She could hardly wait for the never-ending

That One Time My Mother-in-Law Kidnapped My Husband

summer, even though she would miss the snow.

Their mom and dad walked behind them and met them at the door to unlock and open the next chapter in their lives. Pushing past them and almost falling through the door, Tanyah and Renee ran inside to explore. Their parents gave them the unofficial tour and let Tanyah pick between the three bedrooms on the opposite side of the house from the master bedroom. She picked the one facing towards the backyard since she was outdoorsy and liked the view of undeveloped land as opposed to the view of the front yard in the room facing the street.

After about twenty minutes they'd looked over the house and were ready to head back to their family friend's house where they were staying until all of the furniture arrived. Tanyah headed out the door first, skipping to the car in the driveway and looking at her feet. She had not been able to get over the excitement of having clear, sparkle jelly sandals and was always checking them out. As she looked up to avoid running into the car, she stopped dead in her tracks and froze.

Across the street, there was a maroon-bricked house with a large tree in the front yard and bushes around the front door and windows. Standing outside watering the bushes was a brown-skinned boy with the "box" hairstyle. Behind him, leaning against the door frame, was a shorter, light-skinned boy with the same hairstyle. The one with the water hose was wearing Cross Colours jeans and a red t-shirt.

Tanyah's family joined her outside, still chatting with her little sister about the house. Her dad, being the overly friendly man he was, looked in the direction that Tanyah was stuck, waved to the two boys across the street, and yelled, "Hey, how y'all doing!" absolutely embarrassing her, until the tall boy

PROLOGUE: Love at First Sight

looked up.

"Hey, we're good!" the boy waved back, and the shorter boy said, "Hey," but without much enthusiasm.

Tanyah's heart was beating so hard she thought she was having a heart attack before it seemed to just stop completely. Everything was in slow motion for her like in the movies. All she could do was stare as the boy continued to look in her direction and gave her a half smile. Tanyah leaned against her dad and whispered, "It's a boy, and he lives across the street!"

"Oh, Lord. Here we go," her mom rolled her eyes and her little sister laughed.

Tanyah could finally move and looked at them all with the most serious face she'd ever made before she spoke slowly as if they were dumb.

"That's my future husband, and we're getting married," she stated matter-of-factly.

"You don't even know his name!" Renee said, still laughing.

"I don't care. I love him," Tanyah replied defiantly.

"You're 10, Tanyah. You don't love that boy. Get your crazy self in this car so we can go," her mom said as they all prepared to leave.

But it was too late. Tanyah had already planned their wedding, how many kids they would have, and the color of their matching windbreaker tracksuits that they would be wearing when they grew old and died together rocking back and forth on their porch swing.

Two

The Diagnosis

Her back arched up violently from the mattress as he slid his tongue along her moistened slit and sucked at her bundle of nerves. She was on the verge of one of the best orgasms of her life, the one she'd been dreaming about for years, and he was actually teasing her.

He looked up at her from between her legs and smiled seductively while pushing first one, then two fingers inside of her sheath to stretch her out and make sure she was ready for him.

"Ugh! What in the 'still waiting to exhale' are you doing to me?! You're gonna make me beg for it aren't you?" Tanyah whined, but her voice was husky with want and need.

He licked her juices from his lips and exaggerated a smacking sound before he responded, "I have to. You talked all that shit on the phone and now you're finally here trying to act shy like we haven't known each other our whole lives."

Her breath hitched as he curled his fingers inside of her and rubbed a spot she never even knew existed. She was so close.

"Please," she moaned softly.

"Please, who?" he teased and replaced his fingers with his tongue again, sucking and licking her clit until her head thrashed side to side in defiance.

"Taurrean!" she finally screamed his name as the orgasm crashed over her like none other before. Tanyah held his head to her pulsating core and squeezed her eyes shut as she rode it out and continued to grind on his face.

"Uh, uh. We ain't done yet," Taurrean mumbled into her heated center and then kissed up her body taking her mouth into a hard kiss and massaging her tongue with his own. He positioned his twitching manhood at her entrance and rubbed it around her opening to lubricate it. He pushed in just an inch drawing a strangled moan from her lips before pushing in some more.

Tanyah was greedy for more and lifted her legs around his waist, pulling him to her as he moaned hungrily into her mouth and began to pump in and out of her violently. She met him thrust for thrust until she felt the coils begin to tighten inside of her again and braced for another orgasm.

Taurrean squeezed one of her breasts and took her other nipple into his mouth groaning around it as he found his release. He pulled her back to his chest as he slid off of her and squeezed her tight nuzzling his head in her neck.

Tanyah smiled and her stomach did flips as she thought about what had just happened. She stifled a giggle as she tried to keep from kicking her feet and throwing fist pumps in the air. They'd finally done it.

Tanyah giggled as she reminisced about their first time having sex. She was still in awe and as giddy as a schoolgirl even after being with him for almost a year now.

That One Time My Mother-in-Law Kidnapped My Husband

They had gone their separate ways after going to college together their freshman year and got married to different people. They both had kids, and then both got divorced. But Taurrean and Tanyah finally found their way back to each other after not seeing one another or even speaking for almost fifteen years.

Tanyah had loved him for what seemed like her whole life. Growing up and living across the street from him had been a frustrating adventure, but they were like best friends and never took it any further than that. Tanyah did give some vague hints in high school; but, of course, boys were stupid, so he never caught them.

She knew in her heart that they would one day be together, she just didn't know how; especially after they had both gotten married. It was kind of funny though; because they had both gotten married around the same time and then had also both gotten divorced around the same time as well. It's like their hearts were still connected after all those years and were just making plans of their own. And both of their exes sucked, so there was that too.

Tanyah hadn't kept in touch with him, but their younger sisters were still in contact and every now and then she reached out to his sister, Sharee, just to say hello and to see how the rest of the family was doing. Tanyah always told her to make sure that she told everyone hello *except* for Taurrean so that he would know she wasn't hoping he was doing well at all (since he wasn't with her like he should have been). Petty, but it worked. One day he called Tanyah out of the blue after getting her number from Sharee just to tell her how messed up it was that she refused to acknowledge him, and they had been inseparable ever since.

The Diagnosis

It was a long-distance relationship, with her in Texas and him in Georgia, since his parents had moved in the middle of their college years, but they had found a way to make it work. She was currently spending the last part of her summer in Georgia with him and had brought her twin daughters with her to meet him and his two boys.

The kids were getting along like they'd been brothers and sisters all along and were having the time of their lives. Tanyah's heart was full. She finally had everything she'd ever wanted, except for a crazy ex-husband that just wouldn't go away. She sighed contentedly as she stroked Taurrean's back while he lay in her lap.

The whole family, including his mom, dad, and sister, had gone to Six Flags earlier that day and everyone was exhausted except for the kids who were now playing Mortal Kombat on the Xbox. Taurrean had been complaining about his stomach feeling bloated and said that it was bothering him after riding a few rides that day, but everyone pretty much chalked it up to the sun since it was over one hundred degrees that afternoon.

Taurrean tossed and turned all night; and, when his alarm went off for work at 4 am, he shut it off. She vaguely remembered hearing him pad to the restroom and call off from work. Tanyah was just glad he shut the alarm off after the first time it went off instead of hitting snooze his usual five or six times. She typically got up a little while after he left for work to go running in the mornings and his foolishness with the alarm had been cutting into her sleep time.

"You good?" she turned and asked sleepily.

"Yeah. Just taking off work. Close your eyes and go back to sleep."

"What time is it?"

That One Time My Mother-in-Law Kidnapped My Husband

"Like 4:15 am; go back to sleep."

"Oh, okay. I'm getting up at 5:45 am to go run before it gets too hot."

"Okay," he replied as he yawned and wrapped an arm around her tight.

After Tanyah ran her daily three miles, she showered and then sat in the living room watching TV and drinking some coffee before all of the kids woke up. They'd stayed up late playing and eventually had to be forced to go to bed against their will, so she figured they would be up around 8 am.

She fell asleep on the couch watching reruns of The Jamie Foxx Show and was rudely awakened by four kids hovering over her body, smiling in her face, and trying unsuccessfully not to laugh. Tanyah shook her head and laughed.

"Why are y'all such creepers?!" she yelled as she got up to chase them all away and start on breakfast.

As mid-morning came around, Taurrean still hadn't gotten out of bed to eat. She went into the room to check on him again and made him get up.

"I'm not really hungry. My stomach is bothering me on the left side for some reason. I think it's bloated. Maybe I'm constipated or something."

"I dunno. You were in the bathroom yesterday a few times so it's not that," Tanyah said as she thought about what could be the problem. "Come lay on the couch in the living room and let's see how you feel later on."

Taurrean nodded and then rushed to the bathroom. She heard him heave and then begin to throw up.

"Babe! Are you okay?!" Tanyah yelled as she ran after him to the bathroom.

"I must be getting sick or something. I think it was just too

The Diagnosis

hot outside yesterday and I probably shouldn't have gotten my old ass on all of those rides," he replied and smiled, trying to hide the grimace that Tanyah caught out of the corner of her eye.

"Okay, well come out to the living room and just chill and rest. I cooked and got the kids fed already. I'm going to take them out to the park and stuff for a little while since it's nice out and then we'll be back to check on you."

"I'll be on the couch then. See y'all later. I love you," he replied.

"I love you too."

Tanyah stayed at the park for a couple of hours, texting and checking on Taurrean the whole time. The kids also video-called him to show off all of their tricks and flips on the jungle gym equipment. He was shocked at how fast Tanyah's twins had turned his boys into daredevils. Normally his kids played it safe, but the twins were on a whole other level of danger.

Kayla and Kaylyn were outside kids through and through. They ran everywhere, jumped off of everything possible, and made noise all day. They were about a year and a half older than Evan, who was two years older than Javier. All four of them got along great, and since there wasn't a huge age difference they had a lot in common and liked a lot of the same TV shows, video games, etc.

Tanyah had the twins make them all sandwiches and snacks when they returned so that she could sit and check on Taurrean. He still wasn't feeling well, and his stomach was looking enlarged on one side. He'd also thrown up a few times since she'd been gone.

"I think you should go to the doctor," Tanyah suggested.

"Naw, I'll be good. I just need to rest some more."

That One Time My Mother-in-Law Kidnapped My Husband

"You've been doing that since yesterday and I think you're just getting worse."

"Let's just see how I feel in another hour or so."

"If you don't go, I'm going to call your mom. Matter-of-fact, I'm gonna call her and your sister anyway and tell them to come back so we can go," Tanyah said with her hand on her hip.

His mom was a lot. Over the top, over-concerned, and loud for absolutely no reason. Like in the stereotypical black woman loud. But Tanyah loved her to death. She'd loved Evelyn like a bonus mom since she was a kid and never really gave her strong personality a second thought. But she knew if she threatened to call her then Taurrean would jump and do whatever she wanted him to do just to avoid having to hear his mom's mouth.

Tanyah stifled a laugh as her phone rang and she saw Evelyn's contact appear on the screen. It was like the lady just knew when her name was in someone's mouth. Or maybe she had cameras stashed in the house. But really, she called so often it was inevitable. Interestingly enough, she was calling from her car to let them know that she was on her way to "check" on them. Which meant that she had probably left over thirty minutes ago without telling them she was coming and was now already around the corner. The family needed some boundaries, but that wasn't Tanyah's business.

When she pulled up a few minutes later, Tanyah explained what was going on. She intended to take Taurrean up to the ER herself, but his mom insisted that she take him and Tanyah stay behind with the kids.

"Okay, I'll just come up there as soon as Sharee gets back and can take over with the kids then," Tanyah conceded and

The Diagnosis

then kissed him quickly on the lips as they left.

Sharee returned an hour or so later and Tanyah sent Taurrean a text letting him know that she was on her way. They'd been in the ER for a while and hadn't sent any updates, so she figured no news was good news. Plus, she was sure it was just heat exhaustion or maybe even food poisoning from one of the different vendors that they'd eaten from while at the theme park. She made a mental note to check on the licensing requirements because if it was food poisoning, they were about to get rich. Or more likely just some free tickets to come back, which was cool with her because having four kids to entertain was expensive as hell.

Tanyah pulled into the nearly empty parking lot and quickly went inside to find the room. Her smile faltered a bit as she walked in to find somber-looking faces. Taurrean was just staring up at the ceiling.

She quickly schooled her features, putting on her brightest signature smile, and walked over to his hospital bed kissing him lightly on the cheek.

"So, what's going on? Is it food poisoning or something?" Tanyah asked, looking back and forth between him and Evelyn.

Taurrean took a deep breath but then began to shake his head and looked back up to the ceiling. His mom took that as her cue to speak instead and started speaking in a matter-of-fact tone devoid of all emotion.

"Well. The doctors ran some tests. Right now, his spleen is enlarged and that's what's causing him so much stomach pain and swelling, so they're currently taking care of that."

Tanyah nodded slowly and said, "Okay," wondering why it seemed like they were being a bit dramatic over something that appeared to be fixable as she continued.

"But they did run some other tests and they found cancer."

Tanyah tried to nonchalantly widen her stance to keep her knees from buckling and glanced at Taurrean, who was still staring up at the ceiling and now had tears running down the sides of his face.

"Taurrean has leukemia, which is a bone cancer."

I fucking know what leukemia is! Tanyah shouldn't have been upset at something as small and normal as being explained what the diagnosis was, but something in her tone had irked her and she didn't like being talked down to. But this wasn't about her, and she needed to get her shit together.

"Alright, so what's our treatment plan?" Tanyah switched to her take-charge persona and stepped closer to his bed. His mother started explaining what the doctor had told them as Tanyah kissed his tears away and squeezed his hand.

"Why me?" Taurrean asked no one in particular, "I don't do nothing to nobody. I don't deserve this. Why do I have to be the one to have cancer?"

Tanyah's heart tightened inside her chest as she spoke, "We'll never get answers to those types of questions, but you're going to be okay. We seem to have caught this early, the doctors have a plan, and God's got this." She gave him a smile and a kiss on the lips.

His mom offered more encouragement and then low-key moved Tanyah to the side to continue talking to her son. Tanyah used that to excuse herself to the restroom and told them that she'd be right back.

Tanyah locked the bathroom door and leaned back on it to steady herself. She slid down crying as her legs slowly started to give out. She didn't have a pep talk for herself and was beginning to panic. They'd just found each other again after

The Diagnosis

all these years. They were finally together. Life could not be that cruel. She was already 0-1 for marriages, no way would God give her another 'L', right? Right?!

She felt the bile rising in her throat and rushed over to the toilet before it came up. Tanyah couldn't even remember what she ate earlier, but whatever it was, came up horribly thick and was getting stuck in her mouth as she gagged, spit, and hurled some more. A knock on the door came while she was barfing, and she willed herself to get the rest out in case someone else had an emergency.

"Hold on a second," she managed to say.

"It's me, can I come in?" she heard his mom ask from the other side of the door.

"Yes, let me get the door real quick," Tanyah replied as she reached back to unlock the door and then moved to the sink to wash her face and mouth.

"He's frustrated and upset. He's been crying and he's feeling helpless. Don't go back there like this. He doesn't need to see you like that," Evelyn said to her pointedly.

"I'm good. I just needed a quick minute. I'll be fine. I'm coming," Tanyah stared back at her, unwilling to appear any weaker than she already felt.

Tanyah finished wiping her face with a paper towel and gargled some water in her mouth. She followed Evelyn back to the room and entered with a small smile. The doctor entered and introduced herself, giving them some more information and the next steps regarding his transfer to the actual hospital.

Evelyn wanted to accompany him and make sure he got settled, plus she wanted his sister to follow and meet them as well. Tanyah agreed to go home and stay with the kids until they got settled and then would go to the hospital and stay

That One Time My Mother-in-Law Kidnapped My Husband

the night after his mom and sister returned if visitors were allowed.

It was early evening when she left but it was still light outside since it was summer. Tanyah needed to talk to someone and clear her head. She stopped at the Dollar Store and parked in front. She sent Sharee a text saying that she was on her way back but was stopping at the store real quick so that she wouldn't wonder what was keeping her so long.

Tanyah took a deep breath and called her homeboy, Kenny.

"What's good, Bizzle?" he answered, using the nickname he'd given her in college.

"Hey," was all Tanyah could get out.

"What's wrong? You still in Georgia?"

"Yeah. Taurrean got sick. He has cancer. Like out of nowhere."

"Damn. You good?"

"I don't know. I barfed at the hospital. I mean, I think I'm good. The doctor seems to believe we caught it early enough and that he'll be okay, but I'm just... I don't know," she choked out.

"Hey, man. That's old dude you've been knowing forever, right? He'll be aight. How's he doing right now though?"

"He doesn't even look sick. Not like cancer sick anyway, if that's a thing. He's pretty upset though and really questioning everything in life right now. I don't really know what else I can say or do."

"You got this, just be there. Y'all gone be good. When you gotta come back to Texas?"

"It's summer so I can stay a few more weeks if I need to; so, I'll be here at least another two weeks. Hopefully, everything will be under control by then."

The Diagnosis

"Okay, cool. Well, just keep me updated then."

"Alright, I will. I gotta run into the store and then get back."

"Bet. I'll holla."

"Later," Tanyah said as she disconnected the call and then went into the store to find something random to buy for the kids. She settled on some ice cream bars for an after-dinner snack and then headed back to the house.

That evening, Tanyah waited impatiently for Sharee to call her and let her know that Taurrean had gotten settled into his room at Emory Hospital in Atlanta. Once she called, Tanyah loaded the kids into her car and headed that way so that they could all see him.

When they arrived, news crews were on site in random areas and entrances were either covered with tarps or sectioned off. It looked similar to construction, but something else was clearly going on. The route to where Taurrean was being held was pretty much devoid of traffic and people. The building almost resembled a quarantined facility.

When she stopped at the circulation desk to ask what was going on, a short woman with brown curly hair told her that passengers from an international flight returning from West Africa had contracted Ebola and were being treated at the hospital, so many sections were going to be inaccessible for a while and they were limiting movement between all of the different departments. Tanyah was glad they were being so cautious, but damn what were the odds?!

They all piled into the hospital room and chatted to keep Taurrean company. He was in better spirits and the kids' stories about the park and their dinner table shenanigans seemed to help. Tanyah got permission from the hospital staff to stay overnight and went back to her car to grab her bag.

That One Time My Mother-in-Law Kidnapped My Husband

Her phone rang in the parking lot and a familiar name popped up on the display screen.

"OMG! Girl, how are you?!" Tanyah yelled into the phone to one of her best friends whom she'd had since middle school.

She met Albany in fifth grade and her family lived on the same street that she and Taurrean lived on. Albany's house was five houses down from Tanyah's; they'd been inseparable, and hung out together all the time. It was funny because she was one of Taurrean's "girlfriends" growing up, but Tanyah never really felt any type of way about it because he seemed to "go out" with several of her friends over the years since they all knew each other. That's just what elementary and middle school kids did.

"Hey, girl! I'm good. Just wanted to give you a call and see how you've been doing. We haven't talked in a minute. What's going on with you lately?" Albany asked.

"Man. I don't even have enough time to go over all of that, but I'll give you the short version before I have to let you go."

"What's wrong?"

"Well, me and the twins have been here in Georgia visiting Taurrean and they finally got to meet his boys. They absolutely love each other, it's so funny. You'd think they already knew each other or something."

"Girl, that's so sweet! I just love you guys! But what's up though, you sound tired."

"I know right, they're all so cute together. But we just hit a little bump along our journey. Taurrean got diagnosed with cancer."

"Cancer?!"

"Yeah."

"Oh my God, Tanyah. When?"

The Diagnosis

"Girl, TODAY!"

"What?!"

"Yeah, I'm at the hospital now. I just came out to my car to get my stuff since I'm staying the night and then you called."

Tanyah sat in her car talking to Albany for a few more minutes as she reassured Tanyah that everything would be fine and said a prayer for them over the phone. She wiped the few tears she had shed, told her friend that she loved her, and promised to keep her updated. Tanyah wasn't sure how Taurrean would feel about everyone knowing what was going on, so she asked Albany to keep the information private until she'd had a chance to see how he wanted to approach it and ended the call while heading back inside the hospital.

For the next two weeks, Tanyah spent her time split between either visiting Taurrean in the hospital for the majority of the day or staying the night and taking care of all four kids and entertaining them at the park, mall, stores, or water park to keep them occupied during the day. Luckily, they also liked to just play outside, and Georgia's heat wasn't as scorching hot as it was in Texas all of the time so they could stay outside in the neighborhood for most of the day and still have fun.

She would have stayed for at least another week, but received an annoying correspondence from her ex-husband, Tommie, and had to return early. Despite their court order for shared visitation of the twins, he never picked them up in the summers for his extended visitation periods and when he did come around, he would only get them for the day or part of the weekend.

The twins had called him and bragged about their summer trip to Georgia and how much fun they were having. For Tommie, that provided the perfect opportunity to be his usual

That One Time My Mother-in-Law Kidnapped My Husband

asshole self and send Tanyah an email "demanding" to see the kids the next day knowing that she was more than twelve hours away.

"Tanyah, I will be exercising my visitation rights this weekend and will be at the pickup spot tomorrow at 6 pm."

This was the type of bullshit she'd had to deal with ever since she divorced him. He was unpredictable and only popped up when it suited him or when he felt like disrupting her world and getting on her nerves. Before she'd reconnected with Taurrean, he'd been AWOL for months at a time except for phone calls to the kids, random texts calling Tanyah rude names out of the blue, and/or cursing her out and complaining about the child support that he was ordered to pay, but didn't pay.

In the beginning, when he did pay the child support for about six months to look good before one of their many court hearings, she'd given all of it back to him for several months in a row just to try and shut his ass up, but that didn't even work. It's like he just woke up on certain days and chose violence for no apparent reason. You'd think after being divorced for damn near five years he would have found something more interesting to do with his free time.

Tanyah debated on what to say to try and get him to agree to switch weekends with her or to just wait until she returned for him to see the kids. He hadn't tried to see them for the whole summer; and now, he just had to have them on that specific weekend when he knew she'd be back the following week.

She quickly typed up an email explaining what he already knew, reiterating the fact that they were currently in Georgia and would not be able to make it back to Texas in time to meet him at six o'clock. Tanyah let him know that she already had

The Diagnosis

plans to return the following week and asked if he would be willing to wait until then and suggested that the girls could stay with him longer if he wanted to do that as well.

Of course, it couldn't possibly be that easy for her. His email response was the usual threatening retort: *"I'll be at the meeting spot at 6 pm; if you're not there, then I'm calling the police and filing a police report for the interference of child custody, possession, and access."*

Tanyah tried her best to keep her personal life and details to herself since it was none of his business, plus she didn't need to give him any more ammunition to harass her with. But against her better judgment, she decided to try replying with the whole truth and see if it would "set her free" as the saying implied. It was a long shot, but definitely worth a try given the circumstances.

She replied with a brief statement saying that her boyfriend was just diagnosed with cancer and was in the hospital, so she was waiting another week to make sure everything was okay and help out as much as she could before returning home the next week. She asked him again if he would be okay with waiting and then switching weekends with her. His response came back about ten minutes later. She was hopeful and assumed that meant he'd given it thoughtful consideration before responding in the affirmative.

Nope. She'd been married to a complete sociopath with narcissistic tendencies. His reply read: *"I'll be at the meet-up spot at 6 pm tomorrow. Tell my kids I'll see them tomorrow."*

"Ugh! Fuckin' A!!!" Tanyah yelled into the air.

Thankfully, Tommie always started his bullshit early in the morning, so she still had the whole day to spend with Taurrean before she had to get ready to leave at o'dark thirty to try and

That One Time My Mother-in-Law Kidnapped My Husband

be back in time to meet up with the idiot. She knew it wouldn't normally be a huge deal if she showed up late, but she didn't want to risk this whole situation turning into some nationwide manhunt for her since she was in another state. Tanyah was sure that he would find a way to twist things around and make it seem like she'd kidnapped the kids and run away.

He called the police before, and she had been at a neighbor's house and decided to walk instead of drive since it was only a few blocks away; plus, the kids wanted to ride their bikes to take with them. Tanyah had been less than five minutes late, and of course, when she got there, he told the twins that they couldn't bring their bikes. He said he'd bought them some to keep at his place, but it turned out to be a lie and just another way to inconvenience her by making her have to walk both of the bikes back home herself.

Tanyah didn't bother responding and instead decided to make the most of their last day. She spent the rest of the morning hanging out with the kids and playing games before heading up to the hospital to check in with Taurrean and see how he was doing. The doctors were still doing random tests every few days but the treatment and medication they'd started him on seemed to be working. He was noticeably losing weight, but the labs were coming out better, so they didn't seem to be too concerned.

Evelyn arrived at the hospital a few hours after Tanyah. She explained the situation with her ex and why she had to leave sooner than planned. Evelyn stayed for about an hour just talking with the both of them and then to the nurses before she left to visit with Sharee and the kids until Tanyah returned. She walked her out to the lobby and on towards the elevator.

"I just want to thank you," Evelyn said as she stopped before

The Diagnosis

pressing the call button for the elevator.

"For what?"

"For staying and being here for Taurrean. And for taking care of all the kids as well. I appreciate that, and it shows me how much you love him. I know he loves you for that as well."

"Your family has been my family since I can remember, and I've always thought of you as another mother to me. I love your son with all of my heart. I always have."

Evelyn always treated Tanyah like a daughter. She called Tanyah as soon as she found out that she and Taurrean had started talking to each other after all those years. She would drop hints about her wanting them to get married all the time.

When Tanyah first came to visit, she noticed that her and Taurrean's senior prom picture that they had taken together was in a frame on one of their shelves with the rest of the family photos. She smiled, thinking that Evelyn had put the picture out since she knew that Tanyah was coming.

She later found out from Sharee that she'd had that picture up in every house since it was taken. Apparently, it had caused many arguments between Taurrean's ex-wife and their mom because she refused to take it down and would say that he should have married Tanyah instead whenever she was mad.

Evelyn gave her a smile and a hug and said goodbye letting her know that either she or his sister would come back after Tanyah left the hospital that evening. She stopped by the vending machine to get some snacks on her way back to Taurrean's room.

He didn't have much of an appetite these days but ate a few chips just to please her while they passed the time talking about the kids, their future together, and watching TV. Tanyah had mentioned possibly trying to get the geographical restriction removed from her divorce decree and moving to Georgia.

Tommie didn't opt to see the kids enough for a move to matter and she figured a change of scenery and some distance from the foolishness might do her some good in the long run anyway. With him not taking advantage of his visitation, it seemed as though she'd have a pretty strong case for being able to move wherever she wanted. Tanyah knew that it would be a battle just because it was Taurrean that she was now seeing. Had it been anyone else, only about half of this foolishness would be happening to her at any given time.

She thought back to when she first went home after being married to Tommie. She was still pregnant with the twins. Other than the events that occurred that day, the main reason she remembered it was because she had just gotten some new maternity overalls and she was looking cuter than ever with her huge belly!

Taurrean was still away at college but his dad, Rick, was outside across the street when Tanyah and Tommie pulled into her parents' driveway. She hadn't seen him in a few years since he was still in the military and traveled a lot.

Tanyah half ran, half walked swiftly across the street to hug him in her excitement. Tommie followed behind, noticeably irritated.

"Oh my gosh, Mr. Rick! Hi!" Tanyah exclaimed.

"Hey, young lady. Long time no see. How are you?" he responded while smiling at her warmly.

"I'm doing good! I'm having TWINS!" Tanyah replied with pride as she rubbed her belly.

Tommie subtly cleared his throat from beside her.

"Oh my goodness! I'm so sorry, babe! Mr. Rick, this is my husband, Tommie," Tanyah said quickly.

The Diagnosis

They shook hands as Rick smiled and said, "It's nice to meet you. You have a great woman right here. She was supposed to be *my* daughter-in-law. So treat her right."

Holy shit! Holy shit! Why would you say that?! Tanyah silently screamed in her head while simultaneously trying to keep her eyes from bulging out. She smiled uncomfortably as she saw darkness flash across Tommie's eyes before he half-smiled and said nothing.

Tanyah shook her head, trying to dispel the memory of Tommie's threats that came shortly after that interaction so that she could be back in the moment with Taurrean.

They kept their goodbyes short, and she promised to fly in to see him in the next month or two after she got settled with her school schedule for work. She was transitioning from teaching middle school mathematics to being the campus mathematics intervention coach and was excited about the change in position. It would open up her schedule more and allow for a lot of flexibility.

Her goal was to teach computer science or something related to the field since that's what she'd gone to college and gotten her degree in, but she'd been a part of the math department for her whole teaching career thus far and it was hard to get out of it despite her being more than qualified for any of the technology positions. She ultimately wanted to get out of the classroom and be able to train and work with the technology teachers in the district and form a whole team of computer science teachers since it wasn't a huge field or focal point at the time.

Tanyah packed the twins and all of their belongings into the car super early the next morning and called her parents to let them know she was traveling back to Texas, so they'd know she was hitting the road again.

She got back around 5:15 pm with enough time to grab some corn dogs for the kids and unload the car before it was time to meet with their dad. Tanyah made sure she got to the meeting spot a little early just in case he was there already with his finger on the keypad ready to dial 911 right at 6 pm.

Tanyah waited until 6:15 pm and then called him when he still hadn't shown up. No answer. She sent a text asking where he was and letting him know that she'd arrived on time, and they were waiting on him. Still no answer.

She sat in the parking lot alternating between calling and texting every 15 minutes until 7 pm. He never returned a single call or text. He never even showed up.

Son of a bitch!

Three

The Proposal

Tanyah reminisced as she drove to Pearl, Mississippi. It had barely been two years since Taurrean was in the hospital for almost two months after finding out that he'd been diagnosed with cancer. It seemed as though God had performed a miracle; because, after he got out, he was fine. He had to take a few medications daily and do check ups each month, but he was fine. He'd gained his weight back and was looking like his normal, sexy self.

It was Valentine's day weekend, and they had decided to do a mini vacation and meet each other halfway in Mississippi so that they wouldn't have to waste what little time they had with each other by being in the car for 12-13 hours driving. Tanyah was so excited to see him since it had been a few months. His work schedule had picked back up and her twins were in basketball season, so they both were struggling with finding time to get away.

That One Time My Mother-in-Law Kidnapped My Husband

Taurrean had already arrived earlier than planned. Tanyah was getting closer to their little getaway and running out of new music to listen to in the car. It was a boring drive through the country with signs that warned her to keep a lookout for bears. It was getting dark. Her phone rang and she jumped to grab it, thinking that it was him.

"Hey!" she spoke into the phone without looking.

"Helluh?" her little sister said softly, and they both cracked up laughing into the phone.

"You're so stupid, Renee! I'm about to choke on my spit and wreck this car!" Tanyah said between laughs.

There was a song by Ideal called Creep Inn that they always listened to when they were younger. The song started with one of the group members pretending to be on the phone calling his girl, and when the line picked up, instead of just saying, "Hello?" or beginning the conversation, he put on his soft, deep, sexy voice and said, "Helluh?"

Ever since then, Tanyah and her sister would randomly answer their phones like that when the other one called. Tanyah would even call her at work sometimes and play on the phone because she was just childish like that.

"Girl, are you almost there yet?!" Renee asked into the phone.

"Yeah, I'm like 30 minutes out. I had to stop to get gas again, plus I needed some candy to tide me over until dinner."

"Oh, okay. Well, I just wanted to call and check on you since I knew you were driving. What y'all got planned for tonight?"

"I dunno, probably just eat or something for now. I know we're going to breakfast in the morning. But… I do have on a special little outfit," Tanyah said suggestively.

"You little ho'!"

"Damn right! I have on my long, black fashion coat with

nothing but some cute lingerie underneath and my black high heels. Girl, he's gonna open that door and hopefully tear me up!" Tanyah laughed into the phone.

"Ew, y'all are nasty!" Renee returned the laughter.

"Girl, let me get off this phone so I can surprise my baby!"

"Aight, Sis. Love you."

"Love you too, Ren," Tanyah said as they hung up the phone.

Tanyah pulled her car around to the front of the Hilton hotel and parked. She grabbed her luggage and walked into the building towards the front desk. Taurrean hadn't answered when she called, so she needed the room number. They were expecting her and told her that he'd picked up both keys. She stopped by the bathroom to freshen up her makeup and then headed up to the third floor.

Tanyah put her luggage to the side of the door before taking a look around to make sure that no one else was in the hallway. She unbuttoned her coat and loosened the belt so that you could see her lingerie. She was wearing a sexy, laced red bra with a bow in the middle of her cleavage. Her matching red-laced thong had bows on the side. She wore red thigh highs and black heels that made both her legs and ass look amazing.

She knocked on the door and stood back a little so that he could get a full frontal view when he opened the door. Taurrean opened the door and stared at her right in the face with wide eyes. Then he slammed the door in her face!

"What the hell?! Open this damn door, boy!" Tanyah yelled at him through the auto-locked door.

Taurrean opened the door back and apologized, then laughed.

"I'm so sorry babe, you're early, you weren't supposed to be here yet!"

That One Time My Mother-in-Law Kidnapped My Husband

"Boy. Get this damn suitcase before I beat your ass in these heels!" Tanyah yelled back as she stormed into the room.

She looked around. There were roses on the floor near the bed, and the box they came in was still more than halfway full and laying on the side table. A few candles were lit, and others were still in a box. There was a card with her name on it laying on one of the pillows. Tanyah smiled and turned around to kiss him.

"Aw, baby!"

"Yeah, long story babe," he said as he kissed her and moved her suitcase to the closet. "I wanted everything to be perfect for you; but, after I came in, I lost my car keys and had everything in the car. The guy at the front desk was helping me, and then we thought that I'd locked them in the car. I dropped them in the parking lot and someone just turned them in not too long ago."

Tanyah laughed, "Only you, babe. Only you. But it's beautiful. You know I don't need all that. Now, look at what I have on before I feel insulted!"

Taurrean seemed to notice her being pretty much half-naked for the first time. He smiled and crept towards her, licking his lips. She squealed and jumped onto the bed, biting her bottom lip as she laid back and spread her legs inviting him to taste her.

He removed her heels and then ran his hands up her thighs to take off the thigh-high stockings. She laughed as he put her heels back on after.

"You look sexy as fuck babe," he whispered as he kissed her stomach and untied the bows on the side of her thong. He let the thong slide to the side while he kissed the inside of her thigh.

The Proposal

Tanyah closed her eyes as her heart rate increased. He moved his hand to her already-drenched folds and teased her opening. She moaned softly and smiled, moving her hips up, trying to "accidentally" get his finger to slip inside of her. She wanted him so badly. It had been too long.

He laughed as he moved his hand out of the way and kissed her deeply. She sucked on his tongue, tasting his blue raspberry toothpaste.

"Still using that kiddie toothpaste, huh?" Tanyah chuckled to herself. "Oh! Ahh… shit!" she almost screamed as he took her mound into his mouth and sucked on her clit.

He moved his fingers in and out of her, bringing her right to the edge of climax before she stopped him.

"No. I need to feel you inside of me," she said sleepily before pulling him up on top of her.

Taurrean braced himself on his elbows as he slowly entered her and growled trying not to release. Tanyah smiled.

"In a minute, I'm almost there," she said as she winked at him and began meeting him thrust for thrust.

They made love as if it was their first time all over again. She tried to commit his whole body to memory as she kissed him all over. When they finally made themselves stop, they were both out of breath and starving. Tanyah headed to the shower.

"Hey, we need to eat," Tanyah called back over her shoulder as she turned the water on.

"I mean…" he smiled back as he followed her to the bathroom. Taurrean lifted her onto the bench and put her legs on his shoulders. He feasted on her one more time before soaping her up and then kicking her out of the shower before they missed his dinner reservation.

His phone dinged as she dried off and put on some clothes.

That One Time My Mother-in-Law Kidnapped My Husband

Tanyah wasn't insecure about their relationship, but she was still a woman, nonetheless. She leaned over the bed and glanced at the phone screen and read the preview. It was from his sister, Sharee.

"Did you give her the card and her present yet???"

Tanyah almost fell off the side of the bed as she jumped back trying to act like she wasn't reading his text messages when he came out of the bathroom.

"Hey, babe! I think your phone was ringing or something," she said while trying not to laugh at herself.

He looked at her sideways and then checked his messages and responded.

"It's just Sharee minding our business," he said as he tossed the phone back on the bed.

Tanyah wanted whatever present he intended to give her. She loved presents, regardless of how big or small. Just the idea that someone had thought about her, had her all giddy inside. She looked at the bed again and saw the card she hadn't opened.

"Can I open my card now?"

"Well, um. Okay yeah, sure. I have another surprise for you tomorrow anyway," he said, sounding a little uncertain, but she brushed it off.

She picked up the envelope and opened it. Rose petals fell out and she gave him one of her cheesy Crest toothpaste smiles that showed all of her teeth. She took out the multicolored pink sparkle card.

"I know a blessing when I see one. That's one reason I like looking at you.

You truly bless me. And I'm so thankful that you've shown me what love looks like.

The Proposal

Happy Valentine's Day.
Love, Taurrean."

Tanyah jumped up from the bed and hugged him hard. She couldn't believe how lucky they were in finding each other again.

"I love you so much," she whispered into his ear.

"I love you, too. Now let's go eat, I'm hungry!"

"Oh my God, same!" Tanyah said as she followed him out to dinner.

They enjoyed a quiet dinner at one of the local steakhouses. They had a Greek salad to start, followed by juicy steaks topped with a Creole crab and lobster sauce. Tanyah had a fully loaded sweet potato topped with honey butter and brown sugar, drizzled with bourbon sauce and he had regular garlic mashed potatoes. For dessert, they each had a chocolate lava cake with a scoop of vanilla ice cream since he knew her well enough to know that she wouldn't share her dessert no matter how much she loved him.

They walked back to the hotel hand in hand along a lit path covered with a canopy of trees. It was beautiful outside. A proposal crossed Tanyah's mind on their way back, but it didn't happen. As long as she got more sex that night though, she didn't even care.

The next morning, they got up to get ready for a late breakfast. It was both of their favorite meals of the day so it worked out great that one of the diners served breakfast until almost noon.

Tanyah was headed to the door when he called her back.

"Hey, sit down for a second," he said seriously.

"What's wrong, babe?" Tanyah looked concerned.

"Nothing, I just wanted to talk to you for a second."

"Okay..." Tanyah lifted her eyebrow and cocked her head to the side as he started talking and then knelt down in front of her.

"I've loved you my whole life, it just took me a minute to realize it..."

Oh my God! Oh my God! Tanyah was barely paying attention at this point because her mind was going a million miles a minute.

"...it's just always been you. I love you and I want to make this forever. Will you marry me?"

"Ahhhh!!!" Tanyah screamed and got up kissing him all over his face and hugging him.

"Uh, nigga? Is that a yes or what?!" he said laughing at her.

"Oh, yes! Yes, it's a yes!" Tanyah laughed as he put the ring on her finger. It was a size too big and he grimaced.

"What size is it, babe?"

"I got a six."

"Oh, that's okay. I can use my other little ring to hold it on until we get it resized. I thought I told you a five a long time ago though," Tanyah tried to remember as she spoke.

"Yeah, you did but I was listening to my mom, and she said that you've been making all those cakes so your fingers probably got bigger and that I needed to get a six. She didn't believe anyone's fingers were that small."

"Uh, what? What the hell does my making cakes have to do with my fingers getting big? I'm not eating the damn cakes! Plus, who gains weight in their fingers?! Wow. Just wow."

"She was just trying to help, babe," Taurrean chuckled.

"Yeah, that's always the excuse," Tanyah whispered to herself under her breath.

She loved Evelyn to death. She really did think of her like

The Proposal

another mother since she'd known her for so many years as a child. Tanyah just couldn't pinpoint the main issue. Maybe it was just the fact that she's an adult now, and you see things differently when you get older. Or perhaps her rose-colored fairy tale glasses were coming off.

It seemed like the closer she and Taurrean got, the more involved his mother tried to be in their relationship. She wanted a say in everything. Meanwhile, Tanyah had to call her parents' house phone, both of their cellphones, and sometimes her little sister just to talk to them. They weren't worried about her unless it had something to do with the twins.

Tanyah shook off the temporary funk and looked at her ring. It was beautiful. It was small, dainty, and understated just like she liked. She began to think about how she'd dreamed about them getting married as a child. The dreams were weird though because they were always a lot older in the dream than they were now.

Even after she married Tommie, she still had dreams of her and Taurrean every so often. Tanyah figured she just had to wait Tommie out until they got older, and then she would finally be with the man she'd loved her whole life. She didn't know how it would happen, she was just 100% sure that someday, somehow, it would.

Tanyah thought of everything that she went through just to get to this day. She began to tear up and cry as they walked out of the room. Taurrean stopped and looked at her.

"It's about damn time you cry!" he giggled as he wrapped his arms around her.

She pretended to push him off as she started to call her sister and parents to tell them the exciting news. Turns out they were already privy to his plans to propose and everyone was

That One Time My Mother-in-Law Kidnapped My Husband

laughing about him freaking out and botching the proposal the night before because he lost his car keys and wallet as soon as he got there and had spent almost an hour and a half looking. He was supposed to propose the night she got there and that's why his sister was texting him.

They ate brunch and talked over all of their plans for the future. It turned out that his job was giving him a promotion to become a manager and they were working out the details so that he would eventually be able to transfer to their Texas location.

Tanyah was excited and sad at the same time.

"How do you just propose to me and then send me home by myself?" she pouted.

"Don't worry, baby. We'll make a way soon," he said and kissed her forehead.

They vowed to see each other again in a couple of months. Her best friend, Nicole, whom she'd had since the 7th grade was getting married. Tanyah planned to go to the wedding in Houston and then drive back afterward to Dallas and catch the late flight to Georgia afterward.

***

Nicole's wedding was beautiful, and she cried seeing her friend walk down the aisle. Tanyah got to take a pic with one of the super cute groomsmen that everyone seemed to have a fake crush on. Nicole's cousin hijacked the photo too and they all laughed about it later. She figured she should get the fan-girling out of the way since she would soon be married herself.

It all ended up working out because daylight savings time

was on that day, and she gained an extra hour driving back. Tanyah could hardly wait to get to Georgia. She'd found a bridal show online that they were going to attend for fun because she wanted to taste cake for free. Sharee and Evelyn also wanted to go try on dresses. Tanyah wasn't all that thrilled or even ready to do the whole dress thing yet because her own family wouldn't be there, but she didn't want to spoil their excitement, so she obliged.

The trip went by too fast, but she had a bunch of photos from the bridal expo that they'd taken together and several more of some dresses she'd tried on at the request of her soon-to-be mother-in-law. She wouldn't let Taurrean see any of them so as not to spoil the image she wanted him to see in his head when he thought about her walking down the aisle.

None were the style that she'd been thinking about, and they all seemed too "safe" or "good-girlish" for her style. They brought tears to his mother's and sister's eyes though, so Tanyah just smiled and played along while posing for each photo they took.

They were pretty. But Tanyah wanted to show more cleavage and flaunt her curves and body when she got married. She'd had twins but was also a former college athlete that still worked out. She looked good. And she planned to make sure that everyone knew it. Vain, but who cared? Didn't everyone want to look like the woman of her man's dreams on her wedding day?

The Fairy-Tale

Tanyah was waiting impatiently all day. She'd moved her car to the back of the apartments where no one else was parked and took up two parking spots so that Taurrean could park the U-Haul truck and have room for the trailer carrying his

That One Time My Mother-in-Law Kidnapped My Husband

car as well.

The final pieces of her fairy-tale life were at last falling together! Taurrean had gotten the promotion to manager, and they'd found him a matching position near Tanyah. He was finally moving back to Texas. They were making plans for their wedding the following year and Tanyah had already secured the venue with a deposit. There was an elite golf course that her apartments overlooked, and they had the best photo opportunities for what she was planning.

"Hey, babe! I'm here. Where do I go?" Taurrean said into the phone as she picked up.

"Go in towards the back if you remember. I parked by that big dumpster. I'll walk out and meet you."

Tanyah put on her tennis shoes and ran out of her apartment door towards the back of the property. Her heart was beating out of her chest as she saw Taurrean backing up the U-haul into the spot closest to the gate.

She ran up to the driver's side door and practically dragged him out of it. She hugged and kissed him as he laughed and hugged back.

"I just saw you, woman. Chill out," he continued laughing as he added, "Hey, is this a good spot?"

"Yeah, you're good. Why?"

"Well, I wasn't sure because I thought you said that you had parked your car back here and I didn't see it."

Tanyah turned towards the parking lot and looked. She turned around again.

"Dude, where's my car?!" Tanyah yelled.

Taurrean started to laugh at the movie reference until he saw her face.

"Wait. Really? Are you serious?" he asked, now serious.

The Proposal

"Aw, man! No! Please tell me they didn't tow my shit!" Tanyah whined.

"Where did you park?"

"I parked right there," she said, pointing to the spot next to the one on the end, "but I parked sideways just to make sure you had enough room in case you needed two spaces."

"You know you can't do that, right? It says so on the sign."

"Ugh! Whatever, let's get the number, and then I'll call white Keisha to take me. Her or Kevin will give me a ride," Tanyah said as she marched back to the apartment.

"I still don't understand why you call her "white Keisha"," he said as he grabbed some bags and followed her to the apartment.

"You will."

A white SUV pulled up outside and Taurrean followed her to the car. They jumped in and she introduced him to her previous neighbors, Keisha and Kevin. Taurrean looked at them and nodded his head.

"So. I believe I know why she calls you "white Keisha" now," he said while trying to contain his laughter.

"Yeah, my Mom said she just loved the name," Keisha said with her valley-girl attitude, country voice, and a shrug.

Taurrean finally laughed.

Keisha and Kevin were Tanyah's neighbors when she had her house and was married to Tommie. They lived two doors down and had twins of their own that Keisha had raised for her cousin since they were babies. They were a year or two older than Kayla and Kaylyn. Tanyah always laughed at the fact that she was named Keisha but was white and not black.

Tanyah only lived across the highway now, so they were still close friends. Her cousin had another set of twins including a

That One Time My Mother-in-Law Kidnapped My Husband

daughter, so whenever they would all hang out, people would ask if they were attending a twin convention.

Keisha had seen her at her worst and helped her through everything. When things had gotten really bad between her and Tommie at the end, Tanyah had even moved in with Keisha and Kevin until the courts could finalize everything.

They pulled up to the towing company's building and dropped them off. Tanyah thanked them for coming out so late and promised to call her the next day so that they could all hang out and be properly introduced. About $300 later, they were on their way back to their apartment, and Tanyah was happy to finally have her man there.

Life was amazing. Later that year, the apartment unit that was diagonally below her new best friend, Porsha, opened up and they were soon going to be moving into that bigger space. Their kids were all friends and went to school together. Tanyah had met her at a birthday party. Porsha thought that she was friend-stalking her, and she was, but it was a great apartment in an ideal location within the complex. Taurrean's boys came to visit the weekend that they were moving. The kids all had a blast running around playing and even Porsha's two kids helped move toys and stuff to the new place.

Once they'd been settled in, and Porsha had accepted her new fate as Tanyah's best friend, Porsha and her fiancé, Josh, invited them out to dinner at Chili's one day after work. Taurrean and Tanyah met them at the restaurant and sat down as they were already talking and laughing. The waiter had dropped off several glasses of water to start everyone off before the group ordered. They chatted and laughed while looking over the menu. Everyone was sipping water except for Taurrean. He looked around the table for his glass. Tanyah noticed him looking and asked if he'd not gotten water. Everyone looked around the table.

Josh looked around and then saw his glass of water was still next to him and he'd been drinking Taurrean's water the whole time.

"My bad, bruh," Josh said as he handed Taurrean the other water and then all of them started laughing uncontrollably.

From that evening, the four of them formed a bond and they made sure to make time to hang out together when their busy schedules allowed for it. They were family now.

Love on Fire

Tanyah and Taurrean wanted a nice wedding, but they didn't want to wait to get married. Tanyah wanted to take her time to plan and have everything that each of them wanted. So, they set out to get married with just family in July and to save the actual big ceremony for friends and stuff until the following year. They pledged their love in front of their parents, sisters, and kids and were married on July 25, 2015.

Everyone was so happy and excited to celebrate. They took a ton of pictures and then had a mini photo shoot with one of Tanyah's former coworkers from school who was now a photographer. Afterward, the newly joined family all went out to eat and of course, Porsha joined them.

To add to the celebration, Taurrean announced that his job was finally changing his normal shift to be during the daytime instead of the early afternoon to late at night. Everything was perfect in Tanyah's life now. She couldn't possibly ask for anything else.

That One Time My Mother-in-Law Kidnapped My Husband

They spent the Thanksgiving holiday with Taurrean's family the year before, so the plan for this year was to go and be with Tanyah's family. He was excited because he was finally going to be able to spend time with his best friend, Allen, from childhood, whose family also lived on the same old street on the corner. Allen was a straight nut and neither one of them had any sense when they got together. They got on her damn nerves.

She rolled her eyes as she remembered when she and Taurrean were in Walmart, and he'd told her he'd forgotten to grab something from the grocery section. She told him to meet her by the protein, but he never came. She'd left her purse in the basket and her cell phone was inside, so she decided to just stay put since that's where she told him she'd be. Plus, every survival story always indicated that you should stay put and not wander around. At least ten minutes went by before she heard what she thought was a store announcement.

"ATTENTION, TANYAH WATSON. ATTENTION, TANYAH WATSON. YOUR HUSBAND IS WAITING FOR YOU AT REGISTER 16. AGAIN, TANYAH WATSON, YOUR HUSBAND IS WAITING FOR YOU AT REGISTER 16."

Tanyah looked up at the intercom in the ceiling and glared her eyes at the person she was imagining making the announcement.

"I know the fuck he didn't!"

Tanyah walked nonchalantly to the register, feeling every eye on her as she passed by the rows, and arrived at register 16 with a smiling face before she flipped.

"Seriously?! What the hell?! You had them call me on the intercom like I'm some lost kid?!" Tanyah spat out.

"Chill out. I didn't know where you were and when I called

The Proposal

you, your phone was with me," he replied like there wasn't an issue.

"That's some bullshit! I told you exactly where I was gonna be!" Tanyah gave him the silent treatment the whole way home.

She didn't speak to him when they got into the house for about an hour while she cooked and put up groceries. She was totally embarrassed, and he thought it was funny. Tanyah walked to the room to get ready to shower and heard him laughing out on the balcony.

His phone was on speaker, and he was laughing and talking with Allen on the phone.

"Dawg, you had them call her on the intercom?!"

"Yeah. Bro, she was PISSED!"

They both started cackling and laughing hard as hell and Tanyah lost it. She busted through the porch door and started yelling all sorts of curse words at both of them. The whole episode was hilarious days after the fact. But again, those fools got on her damn nerves.

After that fateful day, when she was ten years old, when she'd first seen Taurrean and Allen, she knew they would all be good friends. And they were, despite distance and not talking to each other as often as when they were all younger and living on the same street.

* * *

Towards the end of the year, Taurrean and Tanyah had talked, and they decided that they wanted a bigger space. The plan had been for her and the twins to eventually move to Georgia and his parents were going to have them rent their other home outside of Atlanta, but things didn't work out as planned. They

That One Time My Mother-in-Law Kidnapped My Husband

decided to look in Texas for a house to rent.

Tanyah was talking to her cake-decorating bestie, whom she affectionately referred to as Dr. Steff, and mentioned that they were wanting to start looking for a house to rent. Steff had multiple degrees and certifications, plus she owned a few businesses. She was currently taking a business class at the local college and recalled that there was a Realtor in her class that semester.

"His name is Henry. He's really cool. I'll do an introduction so that you'll have each other's information."

"That's perfect! Thanks!" Tanyah squealed.

She always loved looking at houses. She would go around the neighborhood when she was little and play around in all of the new houses that were just being built.

A few minutes after she got off the phone, it dinged with a text from Steff. She'd sent a group text to her and Henry to let them get acquainted. They all laughed and joked for a few hours, and Henry emailed her some properties to look at and choose.

Tanyah went over the list with Taurrean, and they settled on the first house that they wanted to see. She sent a quick email to Henry with the information and requested a time on his calendar to go check it out.

That weekend, Taurrean, Tanyah, and the twins drove over to the house they wanted to see. They were meeting Henry there, but left a little earlier to check out the neighborhood. It was a fairly new development, only about ten years old, and they were in the process of building a shopping center not too far down the road. The neighborhood had a pool and play area that the twins were excited about.

They pulled into the driveway, and Henry pulled up shortly

The Proposal

after. Tanyah got out of the car and walked around to meet him, while Taurrean got out and was opening the back door for the twins. Henry got out of his car, and Tanyah stopped dead in her tracks.

Henry stood around six feet tall and had an athletic build. He was wearing jeans, a black and white horizontal striped sweater, and some nice shoes that she wouldn't know anything about. The guy had style. Henry had a very light complexion and piercing sage-green eyes. Tanyah was holding her breath.

"Damn!" Tanyah thought to herself. Henry was fine as hell. And now she was going to have to kill Steff. She hadn't warned her or anything. Tanyah slowly turned back to Taurrean, who was now giving her a strong-ass side-eye. She smiled innocently, shook Henry's hand, and then introduced him to Taurrean and the girls.

The house wasn't what they were looking for. The inside had a weird layout that wouldn't have worked with all of their furniture. They drove home and Tanyah could feel the side of her face burning as she childishly tried to avoid making eye contact with Taurrean in the car.

"So, where did you meet Henry?" he asked her.

"I hadn't met him before today, I only talked to him on the phone with Steff. She recommended him and said he's really good."

"Uh, huh," he gave her another side eye and she laughed.

They decided to keep house-hunting though since they still had a few months. But Tanyah had to call Steff. She dropped Taurrean and the kids at home and decided to go to Walmart. She called her as soon as she turned out of the apartment complex.

"Bitch," Tanyah said into the phone when Steff picked up.

That One Time My Mother-in-Law Kidnapped My Husband

Steff immediately started roaring with laughter as she said, "What?"

"You know good damn well why I'm calling!"

"How did the showing go with Henry?"

"Why didn't you tell me he was fine?! Taurrean was looking at me crazy as hell when he got out of that car, and I damn near tripped over a crack in the sidewalk when I saw him!"

"What? Ew! He's ugly to me. He's from Louisiana and he has weird eyes. I don't like that shit."

"You could have warned me," Tanyah said as they both started laughing.

They talked some more about cakes and some classes that they wanted to take and then got off the phone. Tanyah finished shopping and headed back home. After dinner, they looked at some more houses online and made plans to go see more.

* * *

They went to Taurrean's family's house that year in Georgia for Christmas because he needed to check in with his oncologist. It was really like they had forgotten he even had cancer. He was no longer on any medication and all he did was go to checkups to every few months. Since the appointments were so far apart, they hadn't bothered to look for a doctor in Texas and he would just schedule his appointments around the times when he would be traveling to see his kids since they still lived in Virginia with their mom.

Christmas was amazing. They had all of the kids together and his parents went all out on the gift-giving. They spoiled all four of the kids rotten and even bought Tanyah a personal

The Proposal

laptop. It was very lavish and over the top, but everyone had so much fun.

Tanyah was happy to be there, and even more happy to not hear Taurrean's phone ringing all day. She wasn't sure if she just hadn't noticed it before since he was usually at work in the beginning and they weren't living in the same household, but it seemed as though his mother called multiple times a day, every single day.

If Evelyn couldn't get in touch with him, she would call Tanyah's phone to see where he was and why he wasn't answering his phone. She had no clue what they talked about, and most of the time the calls were short. It even got on his nerves sometimes and he either wouldn't answer, or he would groan and roll his eyes as it rang. It was weird. But she shrugged it off.

New Year's came and went, and they found themselves having to discuss finding a doctor in Texas. His platelet count was down, and he had to get transfusions in January and February. They weren't worried, they just figured he may have to start taking whatever medication he was on before that got him well. Things were still good. He was still good.

But something told Tanyah to plan. She started consolidating most of their debts together and paying a few things off as well. She wanted to make sure she had access to all of their bills in case anything ever happened.

Tensions were a little high during spring break as Taurrean was supposed to have his kids that week. They had talked and decided that they were old enough to fly to Texas with a flight attendant escort like a lot of other kids did during holidays. Tanyah set up their accounts and got the tickets using a combination of the miles she'd racked up when she

That One Time My Mother-in-Law Kidnapped My Husband

used to travel back and forth to see Taurrean in Georgia and paid cash for the rest.

They had discussed it and made plans almost a month ahead of time and a couple of weeks before the boys were supposed to arrive, Taurrean said he'd had a change of heart and didn't want them to fly alone.

"What do you mean? They're together, not alone. And it's already done and paid for! Where is this coming from?"

"Well, my Mom called. She thinks they're too young," he responded.

"Your Mom called? Of course, your Mom called," Tanyah rolled her eyes, "She always fuckin calls! Since when does she make any decisions in this house?! Porsha's kids have been flying back and forth since they were like two! They do it at least twice a year to go see their Dad!"

"Well, she doesn't want them flying."

"They aren't her kids! Look. The flight attendant stays with them the whole time. You can even walk them to the gate. It's not a big deal and they're not babies. Plus, how do you expect them to come to see you all the way in Texas? Do you plan on driving 12-15 hours each way depending on what damn state you're picking them up from? This is why you have a divorce decree and custody agreement."

"Sharee is getting a ticket and she's flying down here and back with them. My Mom already bought it."

"So y'all just had a whole family meeting and didn't include me? So, what? She's gonna come every single time they have to come to see you? Ain't she got a whole job?"

"Well, now she'll be here and you'll have extra help."

"Extra help?! I've been raising kids by myself since I had their little asses!"

The Proposal

"Well, last time they were here you acted like there was a problem and they thought they were in trouble!" Taurrean yelled back out of character.

"And they absolutely should have been in trouble! I love those boys to death, but the twins would have gotten their ass beat. I took them to the library, and they ran around screaming and acting like they were at war. I took them to work with me to teach my cake decorating class and they left the area and ran around the damn Hobby Lobby. I had to stop class to go get them! We went to the thrift store, and they were running around and hiding in the clothes racks. Do they do that with you?! Because I ain't EVER experienced no white kid shit like that in my whole life!"

"No, they don't do that. And you should have said something before!"

"I shouldn't have to say anything because they're too damn old to be doing it! You know what? Y'all got it. Do what you do. Mine will probably be gone that week anyway, so I'm kid-free," Tanyah said matter-of-factly as she stormed out of the house to go run. She needed to clear her head.

She didn't start thinking reasonably until about mile number two. It wasn't the fact that Sharee was coming with them. She loved his sister. Plus, she loved getting to spend time with the boys and doing activities or playing at the park. They weren't bad kids; they just needed a little act right. Her issue was this constant need for his mother to insert herself into their marriage and have a say so on every decision they made. And really, her issue was with him telling her everything.

Tanyah's parents had a different way of doing things. Not to say that his way was wrong, but her parents respected her marriage. They wouldn't talk to Tanyah about issues without

That One Time My Mother-in-Law Kidnapped My Husband

Taurrean being present. Either they were going to counsel them both or not at all. They would never take Tanyah's side on anything just because she was their daughter.

After about mile four, Tanyah decided that it wasn't worth being upset. She headed home and squashed the issue. When they finally came, she ended up being super busy most of the week anyway, plus with Taurrean at work, everything just kind of settled itself out. The boys were having a good time and that's all that mattered. Tanyah took them to get ice cream one of the days and also to the store so that they could pick out some more bedclothes.

Tanyah's phone chimed while she was out, notifying her that she had a text message. Her sister had sent pictures of her nephews on a field trip, and they were too cute with their little sunglasses on! Trey was Tanyah's actual nephew by Renee, and Jackson was Renee's sister-in-law's son. They were all such a close-knit family though; no one ever made the distinction. Everyone's kids belonged to the whole family, and they treated them as such.

Tanyah posted the picture to her Facebook page with the caption, *"My nephews are way cooler than yours!"*

A few minutes later, she got a notification online stating that Taurrean's mom had put a comment on the photo. Evelyn hadn't met Tanyah's nephews yet, and neither had Taurrean's boys, but Tanyah was hoping that one of these holidays they would all be able to go somewhere like a resort or something, and have a super huge family holiday. It would be perfect too since no one would have to cook!

She looked at the post on her phone and went to the comments section.

"Your step-kids have been there all week and you haven't posted

The Proposal

any pictures of them..."

"Wow. So now you wanna tell me what I can post too? On MY fuckin social media page?! This is some bullshit," Tanyah laughed like an angry psychopath into her phone while furiously typing, deleting, retyping, and changing her mind a bunch of times about what she wanted to say.

She finally settled on a simple, non-combative, and I don't give a fuck about what you're talking about response and typed, *"We haven't taken any pictures,"* and added a shrugging my shoulders emoji at the end.

Taurrean came home and was giving her the cold shoulder all evening and was short with his responses. Nothing had happened between them that day, so Tanyah was at a loss as to why he was in a bad mood. She figured work had gotten on his nerves and he just needed to wind down a bit.

When they went to bed, he still hadn't said much so she asked him what was up.

"My mom called me today."

"She calls every day. So what?"

"She said you posted a picture of your nephews but didn't post a picture of Evan and Javier."

"I'm sorry," Tanyah coughed as she held in her crazy laugh, "Are you saying that your mom called YOU to tell on ME like I'm somebody's child?! Naw, I'm not doing this with y'all. Something's seriously wrong with her."

"Well, she was just wondering why you didn't post the boys and she felt like you were posting your nephews on purpose or something."

"Of course, I was posting my nephews on purpose! They're my nephews! Duh! Renee sent me the picture earlier and it was cute. And? I've posted LOTS of photos of the boys and also photos of them with the twins. You ain't see MY mom commenting on the post asking me why I didn't post any pictures of the twins. So, why is your mom the ONLY person on this whole earth that's offended?"

"Man, I'll talk to her. But, you could have called her and explained."

"I'm too grown to be explaining myself to other grown people. You better tell your crazy momma to stay the hell off my damn page…" Tanyah laughed hysterically, no longer able to keep from laughing at all of this foolishness.

"I got something for that smart-ass mouth of yours."

"Mmm… I bet you do," Tanyah smirked and licked her lips as she crept towards him and pushed him down on the bed.

Four

A Dose of Reality

At the end of April, things were winding down for the school year, but they were still gearing up for the state exams which were being given at a later time than usual. Tanyah was at work teaching one of her classes.

She and her co-teacher, Kinsey, had a great relationship. They ran the classroom like a well-oiled machine and students were making a lot of progress with the additional help that they were providing to make sure that the kids were ready for their math test. Tanyah and Kinsey were close since they spent the majority of their time together on a daily basis as Kinsey was the special education teacher assigned to Tanyah's classes. Tanyah even requested that they be able to stay together when she got the promotion from being just a regular math teacher and became the math coach on campus. Kinsey had her back on everything.

Tanyah's phone rang during class.

That One Time My Mother-in-Law Kidnapped My Husband

"Hey, Kinsey. I think I gotta take this. Hold it down real quick," Tanyah said as she answered the call and stepped out into the hallway.

"Hello?"

"Hi, Mrs. Watson?"

"Yes, this is Tanyah. Who's calling?"

"Tanyah, this is Doctor Campbell. Your husband came in for his check-up today during his break at work."

"Yes? Is everything okay?"

"We need you to come to the hospital now. He's going to be admitted today. Here's the address…"

Tanyah rushed back into the classroom to find something to write with and feverishly scribbled the address onto a scratch piece of paper that she ripped from a student's binder. Kinsey tilted her head to the side and looked at Tanyah who seemed to be unraveling right in front of her. She pulled her back out to the hallway.

"Hey, what's going on? You look like you're gonna throw up," Kinsey said with genuine concern.

"Hell, I might. Taurrean's being admitted to the hospital. They said I have to come now. Can you stay and cover?" Tanyah said quickly.

"Of course. Call me later."

Tanyah grabbed her belongings and told the kids not to act crazy and that she'd see them tomorrow. She stopped by the main office and told them what was going on and that Kinsey was fine covering the classes for the remainder of the day.

Tanyah got into the car and put her head on the steering wheel to calm down.

"This is still your fairy tale. You're in control. Get your shit together."

A Dose of Reality

Tanyah sat up and pulled out of the parking lot heading to the Baylor Scott & White Medical Center in Grapevine.

Tanyah arrived at the hospital and quickly found out where they were keeping Taurrean.

"Hey, babe. What's going on?" Tanyah asked carefully, trying not to give away the fact that she was freaking the hell out.

The doctor walked in right then and, before he could respond, she began explaining that his blood platelet levels were low, and he'd been keeping the fact that he wasn't feeling well from her. Tanyah immediately turned to him and shot daggers in his direction with her eyes. The cancer was back, it was aggressive, and the doctor said that he needed to start chemotherapy right away.

The doctor went over her plans for him and let them know that Tanyah would need to follow him over to the Baylor Scott & White T. Boone Pickens Cancer Hospital in Dallas after they left the appointment. She didn't want him driving himself, but he insisted he was fine. The doctor insisted they go straight to the hospital, so stopping at home to have sex real quick was out of the question when Tanyah playfully asked, even though she was dead serious.

Taurrean called Tanyah from the car once they were on their way.

"It's gonna be okay, babe," he spoke into the phone with confidence.

"I know. Hopefully, it will just be a few weeks or so like when it first happened."

"Prayerfully. Okay, I need to call my job and let them know what's going on and then my family."

"Okay, I need to call Porsha so she can grab the girls from the bus stop when she gets her kids after school and then call my parents as well so they can help if we need it since they're closer. I love you."

"Love you, too," he replied as they ended the call.

Tanyah dialed Porsha first.

"Hey, girl. What's up?" she said as she answered the phone.

"Hey. Can you grab the twins today when you get Braydon and Bianca after school?"

"Of course. You know they're my second set of kids anyway. What's going on?"

"Taurrean's cancer came back. He's being admitted into the hospital, and he'll be starting chemotherapy."

"Oh, no. Tawnie, are you okay?"

"Yeah. Yeah, I'm fine. I mean no, but yeah, it's cool."

"Girl. No. What do you need?"

"Just get the girls for now and then we'll need to get his car back to the house later."

"Okay, let me know when. Josh and I will take care of it."

"Thanks so much. I'll call you later then," Tanyah said as they both hung up.

Tanyah called her parents next and let them know what was going on. They let her know that they were only a drive away and would come if she needed them. They all prayed and then she told them she'd call back with more information once they got settled into the hospital.

Once they got there they had to go through a lengthy check-in process before being assigned a room. The nurses gave him the option to stay in comfortable clothing instead of the hospital gown. Tanyah told him that she would bring some clothes and stuff from home that evening and she would also stay with him that night if Porsha didn't have any problem with keeping the twins. She knew she wouldn't mind, but

A Dose of Reality

Tanyah never wanted to assume and make plans with anyone's time.

The nurses said that the doctor would be in to see him in the morning and discuss the next steps in more detail. In the meantime, they had to get his IV and port started, grab all of his vitals, and complete a blood workup. Taurrean told Tanyah that he would be fine for now and had her head back home to grab clothes and check in on the twins. She prayed the whole drive home.

"Lord, please heal him again."

"There's no way You brought us together after all of this time, just for me to lose him," Tanyah whispered to herself, "I don't believe that. I can't."

Tanyah took off work the following day so that she could be there when the doctor arrived. Dr. Campbell discussed all of the side effects of chemotherapy with them and said that she would be starting with 3-4 cycles of treatment and then she wanted to do a bone marrow transplant.

"One of the things that I have to make you aware of is that after chemotherapy it may be difficult or impossible to conceive children. But we can collect and store your sperm if you're thinking about having children," the doctor informed them.

Taurrean and Tanyah looked at each other and both laughed as though the doctor had told the joke of the century.

"I have twin daughters and he has two boys. Unless there's another type of kid we can have, I think we're good," Tanyah said while still laughing.

"Oh, yes. Okay, I see," the doctor returned their laughter.

Tanyah grew serious and asked, "So, how long will he have to stay in the hospital? When he was first diagnosed he was only there for barely a month and maybe a couple of weeks after that. What are we looking at for this?"

"Well, that is going to depend on his body, but I suspect at the very least it will be about three months before he can go home. Once we complete the chemotherapy and we're confident that the cancer cells are gone, then we will do the bone marrow transplant. I'll need to test your family for the best match as soon as they can get here because using your cells is not an option."

"Can I donate? He can have all of whatever it is, I don't care," Tanyah stated firmly.

"I'm sorry, but your auto-immune disease rules you out right now and he'll have the best chances with a familial match," Dr. Campbell replied.

"Plus, you're crazy. I don't want those crazy cells taking over my body," Taurrean tried to lighten the mood to make her laugh and it worked as he continued, "My family will be here in a couple of days."

"Okay, great. Well, you all just sit tight for now and we'll get everything started. Do you have any questions before I leave?"

"I don't think we even know what to ask. But we'll let you know later if we do," Tanyah responded for the both of them.

The doctor left them and they discussed everything she'd said. Taurrean wasn't too happy about the length of the stay but was ready to get it all done.

"Hey, make sure you let me know when your parents and sister get here so that I can pick them up from the airport. It's only like ten minutes from here. Also, don't forget that I need all of your account info for your banks and work," Tanyah reminded him as he started texting it all to her while they spoke.

A Dose of Reality

Taurrean had his first treatment later that day. Tanyah thought it would be more eventful than it was. They did his pre-labs and pre-medications and then hooked the port in his chest up to the medication bag that was hanging on the IV stand. The nurse said, "Okay, you're all set! I'll be back in periodically to check on you," and then left. They both stared at the bag dripping fluid into the IV line and then looked at each other and shrugged.

They sat and watched TV as the nurse came back off and on looking at monitors and asking how he was doing. It took around 2 and a half hours for the bag to empty itself. The nurse then disconnected him and told them she'd be back again to check his vitals. They checked him every three to four hours throughout the night and he was irritated that he couldn't just sleep, but that first day went well.

Tanyah had to make some phone calls and arrangements so that they would be able to maintain and keep their heads above water while he was in the hospital. She called Henry and told him to put a halt on the house hunting. Then she called her apartment manager's office and asked to speak with her.

She explained what was going on with Taurrean and how he would be in the hospital for a while. As much as she hated moving, and quite frankly she did not want to move to another building away from Porsha, she requested to move to a smaller and cheaper building within the same complex. A unit about two buildings away was vacant and ready for move-in, so Tanyah accepted.

She talked to her parents and her mom reminded her that she needed to let everyone know that they would be postponing the wedding ceremony they planned since only the immediate family attended their actual wedding date. Tanyah knew she'd be cutting it close if she tried to hold out, so she agreed to send the notices. Luckily, they had some great photos from when they were married, so she sent those out with a little note saying that they would send updated information at a later date. The venue agreed to hold her deposit and told her to just let them know whenever she wanted to reschedule. They said that they would try their best to accommodate her given the circumstances surrounding the date cancellation.

Tanyah went to work the next few days and would drive up to the hospital in the evenings and stay until around bedtime. She didn't want the twins to have to keep sleeping at Porsha's house every day and she didn't want them to overstay their welcome. They could be a handful even though they were really good kids.

When Tanyah returned to the hospital she heard a familiar loud voice. Her mother-in-law was there. She walked into the hospital room and greeted everyone happily. Rick and Sharee were there as well.

"Hey, you guys," Tanyah said as she hugged each of them, "Why didn't you call and tell me you were coming? I planned to pick you up from the airport."

"We didn't want to have to wait on you, so we just got an Uber," Evelyn stated.

"Well, next time make sure you tell me what time to be there, so you won't have to wait and pay for an Uber," Tanyah smiled, ignoring her obvious attitude, "Have you all seen and spoken to his doctor yet, or are you just now arriving?"

His dad spoke up next, "Yes, we met with the doctor and she's scheduling a time for them to do the blood work."

They all sat around and talked for a while to catch up as the nurses came in and out introducing themselves. They'd gotten a hotel close to the hospital, but his mom and sister wanted to stay the night. Tanyah left in the evening and promised to be back the following day after work and would bring the twins to see him and his family. She wanted him to be able to spend some time with his family alone since they couldn't stay too long and weren't able to fly to Texas that often.

Taurrean was doing well with the chemotherapy, and his family stayed for about a week. They didn't want to leave the hospital, only his dad would leave and go sleep at the hotel. Tanyah completely understood. So, while they were there, she would drive to Dallas after work to check on him, and then return home so that the twins could sleep in their beds and she would be closer to her job in Fort Worth. Traffic was always crazy, so not having to drive to work in the mornings from the hospital was ideal.

The doctor came by the day before they left to let them know that they would be using Sharee's cells for the bone marrow transplant. Tanyah was responding to emails while they were talking since it didn't have much to do with her. She caught a phrase in the middle of the conversation that she'd never heard before.

"... half-sister..."

Tanyah's ears perked up and she looked in Taurrean's direction. His facial expression hadn't changed, and no one else in the room seemed to take issue with this new information. Tanyah could not remember for the life of her if he ever told her that his sister was only his half-sister. That his "dad" wasn't actually his dad. Her head was spinning. What else didn't she know about this man that she'd "known" her whole life? She didn't want to cause a scene or anything, so she decided that she would wait until they flew back to ask

That One Time My Mother-in-Law Kidnapped My Husband

him about it.

In the meantime, when she got in her car to leave, she dialed Porsha's number immediately. She had barely answered the phone before Tanyah hit her with the drama.

"Girl, I don't know who these people are!"

"What are you talking about?" Porsha laughed into the phone, "What his mom do now?"

"Had a whole kid that ain't her husband's child apparently!"

"Wait. What?!"

"They had to do blood tests to find the best match for the bone marrow transplant, but his dad isn't his dad, so he didn't match or probably didn't even try, and his sister is his half-sister!" Tanyah rushed, trying to tell her everything.

"Girl, did they know?!"

"I mean, I think they did. I wasn't paying that much attention, but when I looked up, no one was looking crazy, so it was weird."

"So, how did you not know? Haven't y'all known each other for like 24 years?"

"I don't know! It's crazy, right? Girl, I'm wondering who his real daddy is now. We're gonna have to play the Guess Who game and turn over all the folks that don't match," Tanyah started laughing.

"Right?! Like, does he have a mustache?" Porsha laughed as well.

"Is he wearing an orange hat?"

Tanyah and Porsha continued asking each other questions from the game clowning around and laughing until they couldn't breathe. They got off the phone so Tanyah could call her sister. She gave her the run down and Renee just laughed.

"Uh, Tanyah. You knew this already."

"What? How?"

"His real dad died when he was still a baby or something like that. I don't remember how you knew, but you did. He even had a different last name for a minute when we first met him."

"Oh, snap! You're absolutely right. How could I possibly forget this?"

"Cuz you always lived in your own little fantasy fairy-tale bubble when it came to him! Making up life experiences and shit that never even happened," Renee started laughing as she spoke.

"No, I didn't!"

"Girl, he doesn't look like Sharee or their dad! They're both like 6 feet tall and he's only an inch or two taller than you! How you ain't notice that? Bye, Tanyah."

"Hmm… I guess I just never paid attention," Tanyah started laughing again.

"Why are you so dramatic all the time?"

"I dunno," Tanyah said innocently.

"Get off my phone!"

They both laughed as they said their goodbyes and then ended the call.

After Taurrean's family left, the next few weeks seemed to fly by super-fast. His chemotherapy was going well, and he was still walking around with no noticeable issues or symptoms.

Porsha and Josh drove up to visit one evening and Josh laughed when he walked into the hospital room. Taurrean was sitting in a chair watching TV. He still hadn't put on any of the hospital gowns that the nurses kept leaving for him, so he had on a plain t-shirt with basketball shorts and was wearing a durag on his head. None of his hair had fallen out, so he was trying to maintain his pretty-boy hair and curls.

"Bro, I ain't ever seen nobody sitting up in the hospital going through chemo and just chillin, while wearing a durag!" Josh said as they all laughed.

Taurrean got up to give him a handshake and then invited them all to sit, while he moved from the chair to the edge of the hospital bed.

They all talked for a little while and then Tanyah and Porsha went to grab some drinks. Porsha asked her how she was doing.

"I'm cool," Tanyah replied.

"How's his family acting?"

"They're not acting like anything. I haven't even talked to them. They just call him and talk to him every day. No one has called and asked me if I'm okay or anything. He hasn't worked for almost a month now, so I'm the only one bringing home a paycheck. I'll be ear-hustling and listening to their conversation and they're asking him if he needs money or something. Like what do they think he's gonna spend it on? Hell, what can he spend it on when he lives at the hospital now? He ain't buying shit at the gift shop!"

"Girl, just give them time. It's messed up, but that's their child. Give them a little grace. A little. They'll come around," Porsha said as she side-hugged her, and they walked back to the room.

Tanyah's parents came up a couple of weeks later to visit Taurrean in the hospital as well and to keep him company. He hated being alone. The chemotherapy, paired with the Benadryl in his pre-medications, was starting to take a toll on his body. He was sleeping a lot now. Tanyah's parents sat in the hospital and watched him sleep except for the few times that he was awake for maybe an hour at a time. They stayed for about a week to give Tanyah some rest from all the driving back and forth every day, plus she still had the twins to take care of and think about.

Tanyah talked to her parents about how she was feeling because it was getting a bit overwhelming. She tried her hardest to reach out to Taurrean's mom and sister to keep them updated and involved in his treatment, but her efforts were always met with bad attitudes and snide remarks. Sharee wasn't as bad as their mom, but their relationship as sisters-in-law was becoming strained.

"I just don't know what to do. I don't have time to worry about their feelings when I'm the one who's here taking care of everything. They don't even seem to care or be concerned," Tanyah told her parents.

"Just keep doing what you're doing. Pray for them, be respectful, and they'll come around. They're probably just hurting and don't know how to deal with it," her dad told her.

"Yes, hurt people hurt other people," her mom chimed in.

"Well, I'm hurting too, and I don't know how to deal with it either but I'm doing it. And I'm not jumping down anyone's throat to try and make myself feel better or anything like that," Tanyah replied as tears escaped down the side of her face.

"And that's because you've been in the Word, baby girl. You have been reading, praying, and making sure you stay connected with the body of Christ. You have people praying for you non-stop and checking on you every day. And you pour back into them as much, if not sometimes more than they do for you. I don't think is family is doing that. And they need to if they're going to get through this," her dad replied.

"That's right. You can say you're a Christian and that you

That One Time My Mother-in-Law Kidnapped My Husband

believe, but if your actions don't show it, then it's all just talk. People know your situation, Tanyah, but what they see when they're around you isn't despair. They see how strong you are, and the hope that you have. They see a grace about you that only God can provide. When you're around his family, they sound like they're in turmoil. And they're probably upset that you aren't mirroring what they're feeling because misery loves company," her mom added.

***

School was almost out for the summer and Tanyah was looking forward to the much-needed break, but she still had to work. She'd asked her parents to grab the twins for a week or two so that they could have some fun since Porsha's kids would be traveling out of state to see their dad for the summer.

Tanyah volunteered and also worked as a production tech for her church. So would run a combination of lights, sound, and audio/video programs for the main Sunday services, different events, conferences, and/or women's gatherings. She loved that job. Plus, it was a time to have fun and also get doted on for a couple of hours by her church mothers. Mercedes and Annie prayed for her and Taurrean every chance they got. The rest of the production team and choir members did the same. They were so loved.

Depending on where she was, meaning the hospital or home, and if she had to work a church service, Tanyah would usually alternate between going to her church or going to her other friend, Dani's church. Dani sang in the choir, along with a few other people that Tanyah met and became friends with through her. The church wasn't a big building like her home church, and they didn't have a huge congregation, but they were very inviting. The small church was located in Dallas, about ten to fifteen minutes from the hospital, and it was in a building that looked like it had been converted from a small warehouse or construction building and still had the garage doors attached. It was a cute little fashion statement.

On this particular Sunday, at the closing of service, the Pastor was ending his sermon with a few final thoughts. Normally, the keyboard player will play a soft instrumental version of one of the songs that they sang earlier in the service, and the lead singer or director might sing or hum softly along.

The chords to Differences by Ginuwine began to play slowly and softly on the piano in the background as the Pastor spoke. Keith, the director, began to hum ad-libs and softly sing small phrases from both the song and the bible. The choir members were all either discreetly looking at each other or texting to get each other's attention.

Tanyah raised her eyebrow trying to pinpoint where she'd heard the melody and looked over at Dani. She had her head down, pretending to shake her head in the Spirit, but was really on the verge of laughing out loud. The rest of the choir members were shaking their heads as well, covering smiles, and leaning their heads back while closing their eyes. Tanyah caught the beat and had to cough to stifle the cackling scream that was about to come out of her mouth as Keith sang, "My whole life has changed, Jesus…"

The church knew about Tanyah's situation with Taurrean being in the hospital and wanted to help out. They arranged to have a care basket taken to him the following week. Dani and her husband also went to visit and check on him in the hospital. Tanyah had some errands to run and a few other things to take care of so that she could sign out for work for the summer. She was happy to finally be off for a couple of months and have more time to spend with Taurrean.

Dr. Campbell told them that the chemotherapy was working, but it wasn't killing off the cancer cells fast enough. She didn't want to risk the cancer getting out of control again and coming back. She let them know that she would be ordering radiation therapy for him to kill off the remainder of the cancer cells.

She warned them that while Taurrean's body had been tolerating the chemotherapy treatments extremely well, there would be a stark difference in the side effects from the radiation. She let him know that he would definitely lose his hair now and that his appetite would most likely change due to his taste buds. Everything he ate would probably taste like metal for a couple of months. His body would be extremely weak, and he may feel nauseated and have diarrhea.

They weren't looking forward to this part of his treatment, but they knew it was necessary so that they could get the cancer under control and out of their lives. They had him write and then sign his name on a blank piece of paper before they took him away. When he returned they had him do the same. It was a little shaky, but not a huge change. They said it was important to track his dexterity or something like that.

Tanyah just couldn't get over how he looked after just that first treatment. Taurrean was in a daze but trying his best to appear like he was okay for her sake. They helped him from the wheelchair into the bed and he laid down, finally allowing the exhaustion to show.

Tanyah got into the recliner and pulled it up to the side of his bed. He was already falling asleep. She grabbed his hand and held it as she turned the television down. Tanyah watched him sleep as he still held her hand. She grabbed her phone and turned on the camera. She leaned back a bit and then snapped a photo of the two of them holding hands. Tanyah stared at the photo for a while and then tucked it away to turn the channel. He was deep in his sleep, so she switched over to the firestick that she'd brought to the hospital so that they could watch whatever show they wanted along with some movies. She turned on How the Grinch Stole Christmas. It was one of her favorite movies to watch at any time, plus she loved Jim Carrey. Luckily, he was asleep, so he wouldn't be making a fuss about her watching it for the millionth time.

Taurrean's mother and sister were coming into town in the next week or so, and Tanyah hoped and prayed that he would be looking better. She tried to break the silence and cut the tension between them before they arrived, but it seemed futile.

"Hey, I was calling to see if you had a minute to talk?" Tanyah asked when Evelyn picked up the phone.

"What's wrong with my son?! What did you do?!" she yelled into the phone in a panic.

"Nothing. Nothing is wrong. Taurrean is fine. But the reaction that you just had is why I'd like to talk to you," Tanyah remained calm as she continued, "I don't know what I did to upset or offend any of you, but I'd like to discuss it, and apologize if that's what it takes to fix this. I've done nothing but love and take care of your son as best I can. I don't understand why you've been treating me like I haven't."

"You have some nerve calling here! He was doing just fine until he married you! He should be here in Georgia, then maybe he wouldn't be back in the hospital with cancer again!" Evelyn yelled into the phone.

Tanyah took a deep breath before responding, still main-

That One Time My Mother-in-Law Kidnapped My Husband

taining a peaceful tone, "Surely, you're not insinuating that *I'm* the reason Taurrean has cancer? That's an unreasonable assessment and you know it. Perhaps, we need to take a step back. You know, my dad always says that when you're upset, you should think about what it is that you're afraid of, and…"

"I don't care what your dad says! He was perfectly fine here, and he should have come back when he got sick again!" she continued to yell.

Tanyah got loud and interrupted her rant, "It's obvious that we can't have this conversation right now and I'm sorry for bothering you. I'll see you and Sharee in a couple of weeks."

Tanyah hung up the phone without waiting for a response. She sat down and put her head between her hands trying to silence the screaming in her head. *What the actual fuck?!* Tanyah didn't know if there were enough prayers in the world to remedy this situation. She couldn't figure out where any of this was even coming from. How could she have missed the fact that his mother was bat-shit crazy all of these years?

She kept all of this from Taurrean. Tanyah didn't want him to be concerned with anything other than getting better. She would suck it up and continue to try to keep the peace by any means necessary. Fighting and arguing weren't part of her style. It wouldn't help anyway; despite how badly she wished she could Superman punch Evelyn in the throat just one time.

Tanyah talked to Dani about this a lot. Dani was always very level-headed and wise in their conversations, but she was also one of those "Try Jesus, don't try me" types as well. She referred Tanyah to Proverbs 25 and would often remind her that the kindness and consideration that she's shown to his family is like heaping burning coals on their heads. Tanyah loved to imagine Evelyn's hair catching on fire and going up in huge flames from what she referred to as her "happy coals" sometimes. It was her way of always staying calm when she spoke with her.

In the meantime, Tanyah had things to take care of. She was starting to get some of the medical bills in the mail and other things were due as well. Her paycheck from the school district was keeping them above water and the extra money she'd saved from a few cake orders and working at the church was helping with little things. But she was maintaining it all on her own.

Taurrean wasn't receiving a paycheck and they were still waiting on a decision from his job on the medical disability paperwork she'd filled out. Tanyah was even taking some of the money from their joint savings account to send to his ex-wife for his boys even though he didn't have a child support order. Tanyah wanted to make sure that they continued to send her something since he always had, but it was cutting into the safety net she'd built up.

Tanyah contacted the hospital social worker and asked her about programs that could help. The woman was beyond helpful, and she was happy to be of so much assistance to them. She provided Tanyah with hospital scholarship applications to fill out for a few donors and other organizations. She even put her in contact with a service that came with their insurance that she was unaware of and that was the best thing since sliced bread.

The insurance assigned her a case worker, and she would be her main point of contact for everything. Tanyah wouldn't have to wait on hold or press a series of buttons and yell "Representative!" into the phone like a crazy person. Yolanda was one of the nicest people that Tanyah had ever spoken to on the phone. She wasn't a counselor, but asked Tanyah how she was doing and listened to her frustrations about the family. She didn't offer any advice, only prayers and hope that it would get better.

Yolanda was able to sign them up for a program that not only gave them a gas card to use for travel to and from the hospital, but also money for parking so that Tanyah wouldn't have to keep shouldering that expense. She would also communicate with the hospital for them upon Taurrean's release and keep up with his prescriptions and appointments so that Tanyah would know what was going on at any given time. Yolanda was like her new best friend.

Sharee was cordial when they finally arrived, and Evelyn acted as fake as ever while she was in the room in front of Taurrean. Once again, they were planning to stay at the hospital and not at Tanyah and Taurrean's apartment. She didn't think it would be a good idea to be alone in the house with them anyway.

They came a week early because his sister had to get the bone marrow extraction procedure started and make sure that everything was on schedule. He ended up going through three rounds of radiation total before they confirmed that he was officially cancer free. Doctor Campbell scheduled Taurrean's bone marrow transplant for his birthday, June 17th. He would be turning thirty-four.

Taurrean's birthday fell on a Friday, and normally, Tanyah would make him a cake. However, with everything that was going on, paired with the fact that he hated the taste of all food except for bland items, she decided to wait and just make one once he got home.

His dad, Rick, didn't come often, but he wanted to be there

since technically both of his kids were in the hospital for this procedure, so he flew in the day before. He wasn't a huge conversationalist but was pleasant with Tanyah that weekend. When he left to go to the hotel, Tanyah left to go grab some more things from the store and to take a break from his mother. The transplant process was as boring as the chemotherapy process, but Tanyah wouldn't complain. At this point, she craved boredom.

When she returned, she brought some communion cups with her that she had stored in her car from church. She wanted to pray with Taurrean that night and had expressed that desire to his family before she left. She walked into the hospital room at the end of his mother's prayer. Evelyn looked up as Tanyah walked over to stand around the bed with them and said, "Amen," while turning her body to smirk at her so that no one could see the exchange.

Tanyah echoed the "Amen" and smiled as she spoke, "I'm sorry I missed the prayer. I brought some communion cups though and wanted us to all do it together. We can keep the prayer short, but I think it's important that we pray and take communion as a family."

"We already took communion so there's no need to do it again," his mom stated plainly.

"Oh, okay," Tanyah said, and then mumbled under her breath, "Because it's not like we should be doing this in remembrance of Christ as often as we think of Him…" as she walked back out of the room.

Tanyah was on edge and wanted to blow up. She wasn't sure how many more "happy coals" she had in her basket. She walked down the hall and got onto the elevator heading down. There was a small garden area outside in the back of

That One Time My Mother-in-Law Kidnapped My Husband

the hospital she'd found that was always peaceful. She sat in one of the chairs and stared up into the evening sky. It was so beautiful out there at this time of night and she could hear the soft patter of water from the fountain beside her.

Tanyah grabbed her phone out of her pocket and opened up the Bible app. She picked the verse of the day and read it.

"And pray in the Spirit on all occasions with all kinds of prayers and requests. With this in mind, be alert and always keep on praying for all the Lord's people. Ephesians 6:18"

Of course, that was the verse of the day. Tanyah laughed to herself and shook her head as she closed the app and put her phone back into her pocket. It didn't seem like God was going to let her off the hook. She decided to call her dad. Perhaps she'd catch him on one of his throwback days and his unsaved alter ego, "Big Boone" would come out.

That plan backfired and she ended up getting a whole lot more *scripture* to back up what she'd already read earlier. But Tanyah did feel a lot better. She sat for a while longer and then walked over to the cafeteria to grab some cheesecake to help boost her mood before heading back. When she got back to the room, Taurrean was alone. The nurse said that his family had left to go eat and take showers. It was rare that they left him alone. She carefully got into the hospital bed with him and put her arm around his body. He'd lost so much weight, but she had too.

Tanyah's way of dealing with stress had always been to find some sort of control in her life. Unfortunately, this manifested as an eating disorder when she was younger. Most of the time she wouldn't even realize that she'd been starving herself. And if she did eat, depending on how she felt that day, she might throw it up. Tanyah struggled with this cycle off and on, trying to essentially cure anorexia with bulimia and then vice versa until something would give, and then she would be fine.

Tanyah pulled her little communion cup out of her pocket and prayed over him while he slept and then took it alone. She talked to him in his sleep, telling him how much she loved him and reminding him of funny stories from when they were kids. She laughed out loud about the time he and Allen had caught her outside on a snow day.

Taurrean and Allen had both taken huge pieces of ice off the bottom of his dad's SUV and ran up behind Tanyah. They both smashed the ice on top of her head at the same time. She ran into her own house crying because she was so mad and then decided to play a trick on them.

Tanyah grabbed a small towel, squirted ketchup all over it, and then held it to her head as she went back outside. The guys freaked out so bad that she had to tell them it was fake. Then they chased her around the neighborhood trying to beat her up for about twenty minutes before she finally escaped back into her house.

Taurrean woke up to her laughing all by herself and shook his head as he normally would. She told him why she was laughing, and he laughed with her for the first time in weeks. Tanyah missed him so much. He was her best friend, but she couldn't tell him everything that was going on. She couldn't risk it affecting him and she didn't want to alienate his family.

They talked a while longer and then she asked him if he was okay with just his family staying the night. They were leaving the next week, so it made sense to let them have their time. She let him know that she needed to give the twins some of her attention along with some quality time that weekend, but she would call him in the morning once the nurses were making

That One Time My Mother-in-Law Kidnapped My Husband

their rounds.

    She planned to also bring the girls to see him since it was his birthday weekend and they said they wanted to check on him too. They loved him like a father and were very protective of him. Kayla once saw him listening to his Beats headphones and could hear the music on the other side of the room. She wrote him a letter about the dangers of listening to loud music consistently. Tanyah laughed for hours at the look on his face when he read the note.

Five

Home Sweet Home

In the weeks following the bone marrow transplant, Taurrean was feeling better and getting restless. His weight was stable, but he wasn't gaining any and was still very thin. He hadn't been outside since the day he was admitted to the hospital back in April. Tanyah planned to remedy that. She asked the nurses for permission to leave the floor and go outside. They were happy to make accommodations so that he could take the machines and everything that he needed with him on the rolling stand.

They started leaving the hospital room at least three times a day together and staying out for an hour or two at a time. He loved her semi-secret garden spot and would sometimes fall asleep outside laying on her shoulder. They walked around the hospital exploring different areas and found a few lounge sections that no one frequented and was often empty. On one trip, there was an art display area set up and they looked at the paintings, clothes, and sculptures that were put out.

Taurrean was more alive and in better spirits being able to have more freedom, but wanted to be at home. He still hadn't seen their new apartment since Tanyah had moved them while he was in the hospital. A few days before the end of June, Dr. Campbell came in with great news. The cancer was gone, he wasn't having any side effects from the transplant, and she was sending him home to recover. He would still need to come in once a week to get checked out and to do all of the normal tests and blood work, but he could leave.

Since his immune system and defenses were essentially nonexistent, he had to limit contact with people as well as his time outside. Tanyah would be off of work the entire month of July and the first half of August so that gave them plenty of time together. Her girls were extremely self-sufficient, but her parents agreed to pick them up for a while so that they would still be able to have some fun and visit with family.

Tanyah was looking forward to being able to just stay home and not drive up and down the highway nearly every day. She called Yolanda to let her know the good news, and see if there was anything she would need to do before they left the hospital. As always, Yolanda was ten steps ahead and had it all prepared ahead of time and was sending Tanyah an email with additional information as they spoke. She was practically running while she was pushing Taurrean's wheelchair out of the hospital the day he was released.

Things were easy while they were at home. The twins were gone for a couple of weeks, so they had the house to themselves. Tanyah took care of him and made sure that he was eating since he was still sleeping a lot. Food still tasted bland to him, and all he wanted was pancakes or cereal. He wasn't gaining a lot of weight yet, but he wasn't losing so the doctors were happy with his progress. They recommended that she give him Ensure shakes to get the rest of the vitamins and minerals that he wasn't getting from food. He was stubborn as hell but listened to her after going back and forth a few times a day.

Tanyah's phone rang and she looked at the caller ID. It was Evelyn. She looked over at Taurrean's phone while he was sleeping and saw that it was on silent and he'd missed three of her calls. She answered the phone with no emotion and was already pre-exhausted from whatever foolishness she was about to hear.

"Taurrean's sleep," she stated.

Tanyah took the phone from her ear and was about to hang up when she heard Evelyn start talking.

"Well, we wanted to come to see him since he's home and I wanted to make sure that was okay."

"I would never tell you that you weren't welcome here. Come whenever you want, you'll just have to wear a mask around him. The doctor says he has the immune system of a baby right now, so we have to be careful. I haven't been around anyone, and the twins aren't even here."

"Okay, we'll be there at the end of this week."

"Alrighty then. See y'all later," Tanyah said as she ended the call.

Evelyn arrived with Sharee and Taurrean's boys in tow. Tanyah was a little surprised since she hadn't said anything about bringing them, but she was glad he would get to see his kids. They talked him to sleep with everything that they'd been doing that summer and he would just lay on the couch while they played video games.

Of course, his mom complained about the masks. The kids

didn't seem to care. Sharee asked Tanyah if she was going to make the kids some food. Evelyn was ear-hustling on the conversation as if Tanyah would change what she planned to say. Tanyah looked at her like she was crazy.

"Why would I do that? They're almost the same age as the twins and I don't even make *their* food. Plus, y'all didn't tell me they were coming. I don't have kiddie snacks here for them. The girls are gone, remember? I'll give you my card and you can take one of the cars to go get something."

"We can get it ourselves," his mother huffed.

"Okay," Tanyah responded as she shrugged her shoulders.

That evening the boys started coughing and having to blow their noses. They were leaving their tissues on the floor while they continued to play video games. Tanyah was concerned. She asked if they were sick, and Evelyn said that they weren't, so she let it go. Once it got late, they headed across the street to their hotel, even though Tanyah had blow-up beds and the twins' room was empty.

Evelyn and Sharee were heading out and told the boys to stay. Tanyah looked at them as though they had lost their minds.

"Uh, they need to go with you all," Tanyah said to them.

"They haven't seen their dad all summer!" Evelyn got loud.

"And all they're doing is watching him sleep! Plus, they're over here coughing and blowing snot all over the place and you know good damn well Taurrean can't get sick!" Tanyah said louder, accidentally waking him up on the couch.

"Look, I get it. But you're coming back tomorrow, and I don't have the bandwidth in my brain to take care of your son and his boys. I'm not even taking care of my own kids right now. If something were to happen in the middle of the night, I don't have time to get them ready or call and wait for you all to get here. I need to be able to just go. So, bring them back tomorrow," Tanyah told them calmly.

Sharee and Evelyn gathered the boys and told them that they would come back after breakfast. Tanyah told Sharee to get them some cold or allergy medicine as well before they came back for whatever they both had going on. She shook her head as they left. They didn't even have their clothes, toothbrushes, or anything. Plus, the hotel had free breakfast and a pool. It made no sense to leave them with Tanyah when her only focus was supposed to be her husband. Maybe she was being a bitch, but she didn't care though.

They all left at the end of the week and Tanyah's dad called saying that they were taking the twins up to Chicago in the RV to see Tanyah's grandparents. They planned to stop at a couple of RV parks on the way to hang out and have some more fun. She was so appreciative of the time they were giving her.

Tanyah spent the next few weeks playing around with her cake-decorating supplies and practicing some new techniques she'd been wanting to try. Taurrean laid down on the couch switching between watching her decorate/curse and watching TV himself. She always loved to decorate when he was around because he always said, "Good job, babe," no matter what it looked like at the end. Of course, she was a great decorator at this point and had been doing it for a few years so everything looked good, but she still needed to hear it.

Tanyah told him that she was going to be decorating their wedding cake since they weren't going to have their wedding ceremony, and their anniversary was approaching. She had some Styrofoam cake dummies that she intended to use instead of real cake since it was just the two of them home. He wouldn't have been able to eat cake and enjoy it anyway.

That One Time My Mother-in-Law Kidnapped My Husband

She covered two tall cake tiers in white fondant and wrapped a red ribbon around the top and bottom of the top tier and just around the base of the bottom tier. She also glued together a few cake boards, covered it all in white fondant as well, and wrapped the same red ribbon around it. She rolled out some red fondant and mixed it with some gum paste so that it would dry quickly and created three red roses to use for later. Tanyah made pastillage for the first time, which was another type of sugar paste that dried faster and firmer than gum paste. It also held its bright white color better than any other medium. She had to make a few batches to get it right and figured out how to store it so that it wouldn't dry out while she was working.

Tanyah rolled it out flat, about a quarter of an inch thick, and cut the pastillage into different pieces using some drawings that she made on cardboard as a guide. Over the next few days, Tanyah had shaped together a small castle on a hill. She used some sharp tools to create a brick texture on the walls and used gum-paste to shape a few scrolls to go around the edges of a few windows. It had six towers attached to it and a small balcony at the top. You could even see an inner wall from the door cutout and windows on the side. She wanted her wedding display cake to look like something out of a fairy tale. Tanyah planned to keep it for show and take photos to advertise her business. She preferred wedding cakes over birthday cakes hands down.

It was getting late and Taurrean had fallen asleep in the living room watching a movie. Tanyah had started pushing both couches together for him so that he could stretch out when he wanted and also so she could join him when she took breaks from whatever she was doing. She looked over the back of the couch and smiled at him while he slept. She looked back at the nearly finished cake and decided to make a push to finish since it would be their anniversary in the morning.

Tanyah started with a white serving platter that she had and then layered the cake board on top along with the decorated Styrofoam cake dummies. She carefully placed the castle on the top tier and stepped back to jump up and down in excitement. It looked good but needed something extra. She remembered the roses she'd made and then got an idea. Tanyah rolled out some more white fondant and created some thin drapes.

She positioned one of the drapes at the top left corner of the cake and then wrapped it down toward the other side. She grabbed the other drape and connected it with a little water and wrapped it down towards the opposite side. She found a few strands of pearls and added those to the drapes for a little sparkle. After the drapes were set, she added a rose to each piece so that the connection to the cake would be covered. Tanyah cried when she finished. The cake was so beautiful, but it wouldn't be on display at her dream wedding.

Tanyah woke Taurrean up and helped him to the bed. He pulled on her a little bit to stop as they passed by the cake on the table. She had the bar lights on behind it, so it looked like something out of a Disney movie in that light.

"Good job, Babe," he said with more energy than he'd had in a long time, and she smiled.

He was awake for a couple of hours while she showered and then lay in bed next to him. She put on a random movie and kissed him. She missed his touch so much but knew that he wasn't back to normal yet even though the doctor had given them the green light to try having sex if they wanted. Tanyah didn't pressure him, but she was as horny as a teenager. It was

That One Time My Mother-in-Law Kidnapped My Husband

July and they hadn't had sex since April.

They talked about nothing for a little while and when it was midnight she wished him a happy anniversary. He leaned over and kissed her forehead and told her that he loved her. He thanked her for being here for him no matter what. She felt like she was going to explode then.

"Can I borrow your hand?" she asked him shyly.

"Huh?" he asked, sounding confused.

She grabbed his hand and began to pleasure herself against him moving his fingers in and out of her wet channel and rubbing her clit with her free hand. She came quickly and smiled as she laid back on the pillow.

"Did you just use me?" he asked half laughing.

"I did. Now, go to sleep," Tanyah laughed and closed her eyes.

* * *

Taurrean's dad, Rick, was going to be in Texas on a work assignment and called to let them know that he would be passing through town. He planned to stop by for a couple of hours and see how Taurrean was doing. He'd gained a few pounds, but his clothes were still so big that you couldn't tell. They were even big on him when he was at his normal weight because that was just how he wore his clothes. They made him look so much smaller now.

His dad looked concerned as he talked with the both of them and asked Taurrean how he was feeling. Taurrean was open about being frustrated with not gaining all of his weight back as quickly as he wanted, and he complained about still having a faint metal taste in his mouth all of the time. But overall, he said he was feeling better and not as sleepy as before.

Rick talked a little bit about his job and then told them about the rental car he had. It was one of the new Chevrolet Impalas and Tanyah had to go outside and see it. It was sleeker than the older models and appeared to have a sports kit with fog lights. She was already in love with the outside, but when he unlocked the car and she leaned in, she almost fainted on the tan leather seats. The dash had a GPS screen that was raised to reveal a secret compartment. This model was now on her radar for when she got a new vehicle.

Tanyah decided to give them some alone time and told them that she was taking a walk to the mailbox and that she would check for any community updates with the apartment office while she was over there.

After Rick left, things went back to the peaceful, boring, new normal of the summer. Taurrean still slept through most of the days, and Tanyah worked out once or twice a day depending on how she was feeling.

Taurrean had a little bit of a gurgling sound in his chest one day, so they brought it up at one of his morning appointments. They found some fluid building up around his heart and immediately scheduled a minor procedure to have it taken care of without a lot of fuss. He and Tanyah were a little scared, but the nurses and doctors didn't seem overly concerned and they expected him to be in and out within an hour. They just wanted to keep him overnight for observation.

Tanyah had all of his belongings as well as her own as she sat in the family waiting area playing Candy Crush on her phone. It was a huge room, with a small wooden desk for the receptionist who was nowhere to be found. Tanyah was seated near the desk since that was the best place for her to be able

That One Time My Mother-in-Law Kidnapped My Husband

to see the mounted television without having to put on her glasses that she never wore. There were only two or three other people there in the waiting area with her, so they were all spread out.

The desk phone rang, but no one was there to answer. It stopped after a few rings and Tanyah looked around. Nobody seemed to care that the phone was ringing and there was no one at the desk to pick it up. It started ringing again and Tanyah decided that she was going to play receptionist that day. She was bored anyway.

"Hello, this is the receptionist desk for outpatient surgery on the third floor. This is Tanyah Watson speaking and I'm taking messages for the staff on duty. How can I help you?"

"Huh?" the voice came through on the other end.

"There's not a staff member here in the family waiting room, so I answered the phone. But I have pen and paper here so that I can take a message for whoever comes back," Tanyah said politely as she spun around in a circle in the rolling chair.

"Ma'am. You're not allowed to answer hospital phones. Please just let it ring so that we know to page someone."

"Oh, okay. My bad. Have a great day," Tanyah said as she went to hang up the phone receiver.

Tanyah laughed at herself as she had to spin herself back in the opposite direction to unravel the cord from around her body. She went back to her seat and heard silent giggles from the people around her. She figured if she at least put some of them at ease with her shenanigans then it was totally worth it.

Tanyah ran out of lives for her game and was bored again, so she decided to download it to Taurrean's phone and add him as a friend so that she could cheat and send herself some more lives that way. She was in the process of finding the app when a text message came in. It was from his mom.

Tanyah opened the message and was about to respond to let her know that Taurrean was in his procedure until she saw that it was a photo. Evelyn had sent him a photo of some girl that looked to be around their age. She was wearing a skin-tight dress and posing with her back slightly turned to the camera while pushing her butt out and looking over her shoulder. She had her tongue poked out of the side of her mouth and was wearing heavy makeup and lashes.

Tanyah wanted to be unphased and act like the girl wasn't cute, but she was very pretty. The accompanying text read, "Look at Jasmine. She looks good doesn't she?" Tanyah turned off the phone and fumed for the next forty-five minutes. She knew that if he didn't respond, Evelyn was going to be blowing up Tanyah's phone so she turned her phone off as well. Evelyn could worry and die for all she cared. Tanyah could not understand what kind of fucked up games this woman was playing or why.

When the staff came out, they let her know that they'd already taken Taurrean up to a room since it was ready so she followed them to the elevators and then down the hall. She watched as the nurses doted on him and made sure that he was comfortable. He was fully awake from the anesthesia. Tanyah glared her eyes at him, letting him know that she was not pleased.

The nurses left, and he looked over at her and said, "What now?"

She turned his phone on, brought up the text message, and handed it to him, "Who. Is. That?" she asked, enunciating every word that she said.

"That's just Jasmine," he responded.

That One Time My Mother-in-Law Kidnapped My Husband

"And who might this Jasmine person be? And why is your mom sending you pictures of her and asking how you think she looks?" Tanyah said as her voice increased with each syllable.

"She's just this chick that worked with my mom. I met her one time when I went up to her job a long time ago and she was trying to hook us up, but she was weird so I said no. She just be sending me random pictures all the time," he responded with an exasperated sigh.

"And you think that's okay? You haven't told her to stop that shit?" Tanyah almost yelled before she caught herself.

"It's not a big deal. You need to chill. I just got fluid removed from around my heart and this is what you want to talk about? Some old photo?"

"It's not old. She sent it today. And you know what? You're right. I do need to chill. I'm leaving, and you can just call me when you're ready to come home. I'm tired of your mom's bullshit. Matter of fact, why don't you send her this damn ring. Maybe it'll fit THAT bitch's fat ass fingers," Tanyah said nonchalantly, as she threw her wedding ring on the floor and walked out.

Tanyah left the hospital and went home. She couldn't believe the repeated disrespect that he was allowing from his family. She was tired of him being sick and using it as an excuse to be passive about everything as well. Tanyah fell asleep upset and didn't even call him.

Taurrean hadn't called her either but returned home the next day late in the afternoon. Tanyah rushed to the car to help him to the house as one of the couples on her church's production team grabbed his bag. He'd called and let them know that he needed a ride home and told them that Tanyah had to pick someone else up at the same time and wasn't available yet.

Home Sweet Home

Tanyah shook her head and thanked them. She tried to give them gas money for the trip but they wouldn't accept it. They said their goodbyes and told her that everyone missed her at church. She vowed to be back as soon as she could.

"I was going to come get you. Why didn't you call?" Tanyah asked as she got him settled in the living room with the remote.

"I didn't want to bother you after all of that," he said without looking at her.

"Look. I'm sorry. I'm stressed out and I took it out on you when I shouldn't have. I love you, even though you're dumb."

"Uh, huh," Taurrean smiled back and rolled his eyes.

"So are you gonna give me my ring back? Or is it in your bag?"

"What?"

"My ring. Didn't you grab it before you left?" Tanyah asked, now panicked.

"No, I thought you picked it back up when you left."

"Fuck."

Taurrean was pissed at her all over again and she was freaking out. She called the hospital for three days straight asking the staff if any of the nurses had found it or if the custodial staff came across it while they were cleaning. No one had found or seen the ring. It was gone.

Tanyah couldn't believe how stupid she had been. She'd let Evelyn get under her skin and now she would forever be able to throw that in her face. She knew that Taurrean would tell her eventually, if he hadn't already. For some reason, he thought that she needed to know all of their business. And that was the problem.

* * *

That One Time My Mother-in-Law Kidnapped My Husband

The twins returned home the following week and they had a ton of stories to tell about their trip. Tanyah's parents were tired. Well, more like *sick and tired* after dealing with her grandparents for an extended period of time because they were exhausting and hilarious.

The twins said that Tanyah's mom and her grandma had gotten into a little disagreement because she thought Tanyah's mom had wiped up a spill on the floor using her dish towel. She also got offended when Tanyah's mom tried to figure out why their Keurig coffee maker wasn't brewing hot enough and suggested that they hadn't cleaned it according to the instructions. The twins were laughing so hard they could barely get the story out.

It was almost time for everyone to start school. The twins would be starting the 7th grade and were excited to finally be able to play sports at school. They played in different select or AAU leagues off and on, but it wasn't consistent, and it cost almost two thousand dollars for the both of them.

Tanyah talked to her principal and the counselors over the summer, and they were able to schedule her lunch and planning periods back to back so that she would have more time in case she needed to run home to check on Taurrean. He was doing so much better and was comfortable staying by himself while she was at work. She usually came home every day for lunch unless she had to take care of some technology needs on campus since she was the campus's technology support person. She oversaw the deployment of devices and helped service issues with the student and/or teacher devices on campus.

Taurrean was still going to the hospital once a week and between her and the production team at her church, someone was always available to drive him. The twins were in cross-country season so Saturday mornings were spent at the meets, and they would play with friends the remainder of the day and sometimes over the weekend. They were enjoying middle school but would still spend time talking to Taurrean about everything that was happening in school or checking on him to see if he needed anything.

Taurrean wasn't an early-morning person and the cross-country meets always started around 8 am so he never went. Tanyah also thought that he was feeling self-conscious about his weight loss, but he would never say. He still had some of his hair, it was just low like a fade. One or both of her parents came to every cross country meet that the twins had, and they usually stopped by the apartment to see him on their way back, unless they took the girls out to eat and would leave after they were all finished.

Tanyah hoped he would get out more since their birthday was coming up. He sat outside on the patio a few times a week, but not enough. Tanyah planned to have a pool party for them at the apartment complex since it was still hot outside, and it would allow them to only be one building away from their apartment. She wasn't sure about him putting his feet into the water, but he could just hang out by the pool. Tanyah wasn't getting in so it would be okay.

Things seemed to be getting better when he went with her to the T-Mobile store to buy the girls their first cell phones as birthday presents. They had been asking for cell phones for a couple of years but there hadn't been an actual need for them to have any. Plus, they always had a house phone. Now that they were in middle school, it made more sense since they were not only in the choir now, but would also be participating

That One Time My Mother-in-Law Kidnapped My Husband

in at least three of the sports that the school offered and had to let her know when to pick them up and if games or practices were canceled. They were also very social so they would stay after school for events that their friends were participating in as well.

When their birthday came around, everything looked exactly how Tanyah had planned. She had some finger foods for them, and her sister and mom were there along with Porsha, her kids, and some more of their friends. The twins had been watching a movie called, Mommy I'm a Zombie, almost every day and buying the themed toys from the store, so Tanyah made the theme of their cake resemble the movie. Renee's sister-in-law also made some matching zombie cookies to go with it and their mom brought them with her when she drove up for the party.

Taurrean sat outside by the pool with them while all of the kids played and ate cake. The top tier flavor was Peach Bellini, and the bottom tier was Grand Marnier. The twins were mini alcoholics already since Tanyah experimented with a lot of different flavor profiles to make her cakes stand out. The alcohol was cooked out of course, but the flavor was still there. Everyone loved it and laughed when they found out that the kids had made the special request for those specific flavors after sneaking some of the leftover cake from a wedding tasting that Tanyah had previously held.

Taurrean was still self-conscious about his weight and seemed to be losing a little more. It was still summertime in Texas but he had on his sweatpants and a long-sleeved shirt so he couldn't stay out too much longer, and the twins needed to dry off a little before opening presents. Tanyah walked him back to the apartment to get him settled in and then went back out to the pool. She called him on video chat when the twins were ready to start opening their gifts.

Their screams were heard all over the entire apartment complex and probably across the highway as well when they opened up their presents from Taurrean and saw that they were cell phones. Tanyah thought that they were both going to go into shock as they kept screaming and looking at the phones as though they had never seen one before. They'd only screamed half as much when he bought them some electric scooters for Christmas, but definitely screamed more when Tanyah attempted to show them how to ride the scooters and crashed into the bushes.

Six

So Close

⸺⸙⸺

Taurrean's next doctor's appointment was early in the morning, so Tanyah was able to take him and have her co-teacher cover the beginning classes. His appointments didn't usually take too long so it wasn't a big deal. Tanyah's principal was very understanding.

That morning, Taurrean had a taste for some breakfast croissants from Burger King and Tanyah was both shocked and elated because he was finally getting his taste back. She was tired of the sympathy eating that she had to do with him most of the time. Pancakes and cereal were getting old. She stopped at Burger King and ordered. They ate and laughed while talking about a new song that they heard on the radio called, Panda, that they could not understand at all. They were taking turns trying to rap the song and basically just making random noises when Taurrean stopped abruptly.

"Pull over!" he yelled.

Tanyah immediately swerved to the side of the road in a panic and stopped the car. He got his car door open but couldn't get his seat belt off before he started vomiting. Tanyah got out and ran around to the other side of the car. She unbuckled his seat belt and held onto him so that he wouldn't fall out of the car from heaving so hard.

"Oh my God! Are you okay babe?! What's happening?" Tanyah fired off her questions as the heaving noises began to subside.

She grabbed some napkins out of the glove compartment and used some of her water to wet them so that she could wipe his face and hands off as best as she could.

"I don't know. Maybe I shouldn't have eaten both of those croissants."

"You ate both? I didn't even see you!"

"They were good," he replied with a shrug.

"You know good damn well you haven't been eating that much!"

"Man, come on. Let's go before we're late."

"I'm telling."

"Babe, they said I could eat though."

"Yeah, but not all of that when you haven't been eating it. I thought we were saving the other one for later. Your eyes are bigger than your damn stomach!" Tanyah yelled at him.

Taurrean ignored her as he reached to buckle his seat belt and pulled the car door shut. She sighed and blew out a long breath. They rode in silence the rest of the way as she glared at him every so often. He blew her a kiss when they were pulling into the parking garage and she smiled back. He thought he was off the hook but she sang like a canary as soon as the nurse called them back to the room. They had to wait a while for

That One Time My Mother-in-Law Kidnapped My Husband

his blood work to come back and were just watching TV and talking when the doctor came in.

"Oh, hey, Dr. Campbell! I didn't realize you'd be here for this visit," Tanyah acknowledged as the doctor shook both of their hands and sat down on the rolling stool.

"Hey, you two. I hadn't planned to come, but I was in the building today when the nurse called," the doctor said to them.

Tanyah lifted her eyebrow a bit and tried not to look over at Taurrean. He was also trying not to look at her as well. As if looking at each other would confirm that something was up.

The doctor continued, "There's really no way to say this, so I'll just state it plainly."

The lump that had been forming in Tanyah's throat expanded and she stopped breathing. She slowly shook her head no as stars appeared in her peripheral vision when the doctor spoke.

"The cancer has returned, but I think we can try to battle it with another bone marrow transplant. We harvested your sister's bone marrow so they won't have to make a special trip. We will also need to resume a preparative chemotherapy regimen for a few days to make sure that these new cancer cells have died off before we do the transplant again. We're catching it early so this isn't necessarily a bad thing. But I'm sorry."

Taurrean closed his eyes and just nodded his head up and down a few times without speaking. Tanyah looked over at him while she spoke to the doctor.

"Can you give us a second please?"

"Yes, of course. I need to go put in the orders and we're going to send you over there once they're ready for you. We'll allow him to come and go for his treatment. I won't admit him unless it becomes absolutely necessary," the doctor told them on her way out.

"Babe?" Tanyah called to him as she moved closer to him.

He didn't say anything. He wrapped his arms around her as they both sat on the exam table together in silence. Tanyah tried her hardest to be strong for him and not cry. Things had been going so well. She thought about what his family would do or say now. Her head was spinning.

"It's going to be okay. I'll fight this," he finally whispered in her ear and kissed her forehead.

He was choked up, but trying to be strong as he continued, "We just have to keep praying."

"Babe, your mom is going to lose her shit. I've been trying to keep you out of it all, but she's going to make this harder than it has to be and I don't think I can take it. I'm trying everything I know how to do. I promise you that I am. I know this is a lot for you, but you're going to have to talk to her. I don't need them running down here and driving me insane. I'm sorry if I sound selfish."

"I understand, babe. I'll talk to them. Don't worry," he assured her as he squeezed her closer.

The doctor returned to go over the plans and schedule again before walking them over to the chemotherapy outpatient building. Tanyah thought it was so nice of her to walk with them and talk to them instead of sending them with a nurse or just giving them directions. She genuinely cared about them and loved hearing some of the random stories they shared with her about their childhood shenanigans. Dr. Campbell was in awe of their love story and how they were handling this new chapter of their lives together.

Tanyah let the nurses do their thing and she told him that she was going to go grab some coffee and come back. She

That One Time My Mother-in-Law Kidnapped My Husband

called her parents to let them know what was going on and their hearts broke for her. But they still encouraged her and let her know that they would still be there for whatever she needed. They asked if she had spoken to his side of the family and she said that she was going to let him call his family. If they wanted to speak to her then she would talk to them but she wouldn't take the disrespect any longer. Tanyah couldn't let their pride, fear, and disbelief cause her to act out of character and not do whatever she felt that God wanted her to do in this situation. She wouldn't be able to make decisions with a clear heart or a level head if she allowed them to steal the joy and hope that she had.

Tanyah grabbed her coffee and a bottle of water. She walked outside to the balcony behind the small coffee shop. There were about five small, round tables with cute black chairs around them. The balcony rails were black with whimsical loops and curls. It overlooked a lush forest with a view of a golf course nestled between the large trees.

She placed her water bottle on one of the tables and leaned over the railing while she sipped her coffee in silence. There wasn't anyone else around despite it being a huge hospital in the Dallas medical district. Tanyah squinted her eyes a bit as she tried to look out further and saw a wooden bridge covering a small stream. She stood there for a while just looking into the trees and quietly praying for her husband off and on.

When she'd finished drinking her coffee she sighed as she looked down over the balcony. She was about ten stories above the ground. She saw a couple walking and holding hands below. Fear crept in as she allowed the thought of Taurrean not making it through this next round of chemotherapy cross her mind. For a split second, she thought about jumping. Tanyah

So Close

stepped back from the rails and looked up into the sky. It was time for her to go see a counselor. She just didn't know when she would be able to find the time.

Tanyah had to put on her big girl panties and keep the show going. She would fall apart if she didn't channel it all into something. So, her something would be micromanaging the hell out of everything until all of this stuff was finally over and behind them. She grabbed her water and headed back to the chemotherapy room.

Taurrean had about thirty minutes remaining and looked like he was out of it. The nurse said that it was because of the Benadryl and since his body was still so weak, it was taking a lot out of him. Tanyah closed her eyes and pressed her lips together in a tight line to keep from throwing her head back and screaming at the top of her lungs. She quickly schooled her features and smiled while she moved to sit in the recliner next to him so that she could wait.

* * *

Taurrean stayed in bed and mostly slept for the next few weeks. They only had to do about five days of chemotherapy before the bone marrow transplant, but he looked really bad. The experience wasn't even close to the first time. He was moving extremely slowly and usually had to be pushed in a wheelchair during hospital visits because he couldn't walk that far without any assistance.

This time around he developed Graft versus Host Disease from the bone marrow transplant. It had caused the donor cells to trigger an autoimmune response and his body began to attack its own tissues and cells. The symptoms were acute and mainly presented themselves as an allergic reaction that looked like he had bad rashes and measle-like bumps on his skin.

The treatment for GvHD seemed as though it was rougher than the chemotherapy. He was getting intravenous corticosteroids along with Benadryl during the appointments and was becoming a zombie. Tanyah could hardly hold an entire conversation with him and had to attempt parroting everything he would try to tell the nurses about how he was feeling. He wasn't eating consistently, and Tanyah could only get him to drink protein shakes.

Tanyah and some of the production team members switched off a few more times, driving Taurrean back and forth to his appointments. She came home from work on her break one day and saw that he'd tried to make himself some cereal and failed miserably. The kitchen was a hot damn mess, but it was encouraging that he'd at least tried. There was Rice Krispie cereal scattered on the counter and the floor. A bowl on the stove was filled to the rim with sugar and the sugar container had cereal in it. Tanyah laughed as she took a picture and then cleaned up the mess, trying to separate tiny pieces of cereal out of the sugar container.

She went into the bedroom to check on him and make sure that he'd taken his medications. She'd gotten a pill container for him that had all of the days of the week as well as slots for both AM and PM medications. Tanyah usually woke him up before she left for work to ensure he took them. If she was running late, she'd call to remind him. He was still good about taking it when she told him. He heard her walk in and looked up at her sleepily.

Tanyah smiled at him and laughed as she asked, "Did you get

any cereal in your mouth?"

He gave her a sly grin and shook his head "no" as he turned over and fell back asleep. Tanyah watched some TV before heading back to work and texting the twins to see if they had a ride home from basketball practice that day.

The next morning, Tanyah got the girls out of the house for school and then went to get Taurrean up and make sure that he would be ready for his appointment later.

"Hey, babe. Time to get up so I can make sure you take your meds and get ready," Tanyah said over her shoulder as she went to the bathroom to put on some mascara and lip gloss.

"Babe, time to get up," Tanyah said a little louder as she poked her head out of the bathroom and saw that he was still laying down.

She walked over to the bed and kissed him on his forehead. He was hot but didn't stir from the kiss. She shook him gently at first, then roughly.

"No, no, no! Wake up, babe! Oh my God don't do this to me! Fuckin wake up!" Tanyah yelled as she continued to shake him and looked around for her phone.

He groaned a bit.

"Oh, thank God! Thank you, God!" Tanyah said as she grabbed her phone and dialed the number for the nurses' line.

She grabbed Taurrean and lifted him from the bed. He was so light now. She half-carried and half-dragged him to her car as she spoke to the nurses and described what was happening to him.

"He's awake, but barely. It's like he's been drugged or something. I have him in the car and we're on our way," Tanyah spoke quickly.

"Okay, good. Just try to keep him talking, even if it's

incoherent. Call us back when you get close or if anything changes. We'll have someone meet you at drop off," the nurse replied.

Tanyah made a quick call to her job and then sent a text to Kinsey letting her know that she would not be into work and she'd have to cover classes by herself today. She called the head of the production team at her church to let him know that he wouldn't need to pick Taurrean up today and explained what was happening. He let her know that he would contact the team and make sure everyone was aware.

When they arrived at the hospital, the nurses had a wheelchair waiting for him and instructed her where to go after she parked. Once she got in, there was a lot of fuss about him, so she felt better even though she was scared out of her mind. She'd called her parents and let them know what was going on. Her dad was always the reasonable one as he spoke to her in a calm voice.

"You have to call his family, number one," her dad said, referring to her by one of the few nicknames he'd given her.

"I know, Dad. I will."

"You know what to do. Keep us updated and let us know what you need," he said as they ended the call.

Tanyah walked around the lobby bracing herself for the call. She took a deep breath and dialed Evelyn's number.

"Hello?" Evelyn answered the phone as though it wasn't the digital age and she didn't know who was calling.

"Hey, I need to talk to you guys," Tanyah said.

"What is it now?" she asked angrily.

"Look. I'm sorry. I don't know what I've done to upset you all, but I'm so sorry. Whatever it is, I'll fix it. I swear. But right now, I need you all to come back to Texas as soon as you can,"

So Close

Tanyah pleaded.

"What's going on?" Evelyn asked as she dropped her attitude for the first time in months.

Tanyah told her what happened and let her know that they were already at the hospital and she would keep her updated. Evelyn thanked her and told her that she would let her know when they'd be coming. Tanyah exhaled as they hung up. She walked back to the nurses' station just as one of them was coming out to get her.

"Everything is fine, come on back," she said before Tanyah's mind could wander.

Another nurse joined the conversation as she walked back, "Yes, he's fine. His kidneys haven't been filtering and removing all of the medications he's been taking. It's just been building up and his body has been too weak. We're going to run a bunch of fluids through him to flush it all out, but it will take a little while so we have to admit him."

Tanyah sat down next to him in the recliner chair and sighed. He was sitting in the bed a little slouched over and barely awake. Tanyah called Porsha to let her know what was happening. She told her that she'd get the twins settled and fed dinner after school and then she would drive up to the hospital later to sit with Tanyah and make sure that they were okay.

Tanyah fell asleep for about an hour while she sat in the chair and waited for Taurrean to become more responsive. She thought that she'd been awake watching TV until her phone dinged with a text message alert and woke her up. She was mentally exhausted. Evelyn and Sharee would be arriving late in the evening, the text read. She really hoped that he was doing better before they arrived. His mom seemed like she was turning over a new leaf when they'd spoken earlier, but there was no telling how they would act once they arrived. Plus, Tanyah still didn't know what the problem was between them or how to fix it.

Taurrean was only a little more coherent when Porsha arrived and it seemed that they were both somehow up to their normal back and forth even though he wasn't saying much. They had a relationship similar to Martin and Pam from the hit TV show, Martin. Tanyah just shook her head at the both of them as Taurrean slurred his words and mumbled, "When are you leaving?" even though it hadn't even been fifteen minutes since Porsha arrived.

"Babe?!" Tanyah chastised him.

"Well, damn. I just got here," Porsha said innocently.

She and Porsha laughed hard as Taurrean dozed off again.

"So, is everything really okay? He's not looking too good," Porsha asked.

"That's what they say, but the way he was and continues to be after almost this whole day..." Tanyah let her words trail off.

"When is the family getting here?"

"Sometime within the next hour or so. I think things are going to start being a little different actually. I'm supposed to apologize and shit, but I don't know what for yet," Tanyah said, rolling her eyes and half laughing.

"You haven't done anything though! What the hell do you mean apologize?"

"Girl, I don't know, I'm just trying to keep the damn peace by any means necessary. I literally thought something bad was going to happen and needed them to chill on the drama this time," Tanyah admitted, acquiescing.

"I get it. I don't like it, but I get it," Porsha told her and patted her shoulder.

The nurses were moving Taurrean to a room that they had gotten ready for him when his family arrived. Porsha spoke to them for a little while before she left. Evelyn tried talking to Taurrean, but he didn't really give her any responses other than a few yeses and nos to questions that those answers weren't even applicable. Tanyah worked hard trying not to roll her eyes or laugh as Evelyn attempted to make him understand her by talking louder. At this rate, everyone in the room was going to have a headache so Tanyah saved him.

"He's still out of it, but I promise they said he's getting better. He just has to rest and allow his body to pump all of the medication out," Tanyah said quietly as she pulled the bed covers up around him to hint that he was going to sleep.

Taurrean winked at her before closing his eyes and she kissed him on the cheek. She hadn't realized how hollow his face was until she felt his cold cheekbones on her lips. She looked at him for a brief moment as her rose-colored lenses temporarily fell off. He didn't look good. He was so frail. The last of his hair looked like baby fuzz on top of his head and his skin had a gray pallor and was peeling. It seemed to be a long-lasting side effect from the radiation that his body went through. She hadn't been seeing him exactly as he was, but not quite as he used to be either. Tanyah was projecting the healing image that she hoped and prayed for daily.

Seven

I-35 Road Warrior

Over the next few days, Taurrean seemed to come out of the fog more. His body was extremely weak, and Tanyah or a nurse would help him back and forth to the restroom when he needed to go. He wouldn't allow his mother or sister to help him and Evelyn, of course, felt jaded as though she was purposefully left out of his care instead of the fact that he was a grown-ass man that didn't want his mom seeing him in this condition, let alone naked.

Tanyah still had to go to work, and his family was staying at the hospital and the hotel that was next door so she let them have the days with him and sometimes they would leave to change, eat, or shower when she arrived. For some reason though, they would never really leave her alone with him. On this particular day, the nurses had given him some medication throughout the day that had him tired but alert.

His family was watching TV while Tanyah talked to Taurrean

quietly. It was evident that his mom was ear hustling on everything she said because when she mentioned to him that their supplemental security income application had been approved and Tanyah just had to fill out one more paper, she piped up.

"What paperwork?" Evelyn's nosey ass interjected.

"I applied for SSI to help with bills and stuff," Tanyah said over her shoulder.

"Oh, okay," Evelyn replied in a tone like she was asked for her approval.

Tanyah grabbed her phone and headphones and went to YouTube to find one of the soft and calming instrumental music channels that one of her coworkers had recommended. She put one earbud in Taurrean's ear and the other in her own as she put her head down on the bed beside him. He smiled at her and mouthed "I love you" and Tanyah said it back out loud. They had peace for about three minutes before Evelyn butted into their private bubble.

"What do you have him listening to?" she asked.

"We're just listening to calming instrumentals," Tanyah replied without looking up or moving.

"Well, I don't know about that."

"You don't know about what?" Tanyah now lifted her head and turned towards her.

"He shouldn't be listening to any instrumentals. It ain't safe. You don't know what kind of hidden messages and devil worship is hidden in that stuff."

Tanyah laughed out loud because surely she was joking, "Are you for real right now?"

"I'm just saying."

"It's not heavy metal. It's just nature sounds and stuff to calm you. The same thing that some people use to go to sleep. I assure you, neither one of us is being possessed."

Evelyn started talking about how people try to trick you online and that she didn't want *her son* to be exposed to it. Tanyah looked at her phone and pretended to get a phone call to avoid the blow-up that was about to happen.

"Sorry, I gotta take this. It's my neighbor and she's with the twins. I'll be back. Hello?" Tanyah said as she fake-answered her phone and walked out of the room.

Tanyah's chest heaved in and out as she made her way to the elevator seeing red the whole time. She waited until she got outside to her serene place to look up into the sky and scream.

"Ahhh!!! What the fuck?!" Tanyah yelled at no one in particular and put her head in her hands.

The only way she was going to calm down was if she called to talk to her dad. She had no clue how she would have survived this far without her parents. But her mom was starting to lose her patience with Evelyn's rudeness and the way she treated Tanyah for no apparent reason. She secretly hoped that only her mom would answer the phone and then give her permission to go back upstairs, punch Evelyn in her neck, and tell her to shut her stupid ass up. She wouldn't say "ass" but Tanyah's mom loved calling people stupid so that would work too.

"Hey, Tigger. What's going on?" her dad answered the phone and she heard her mom's greeting in the background.

Tanyah smiled at God's sense of humor and replied, "Hey, dad. You're gonna have to talk me off the edge tonight. I don't think I can take this anymore."

"What's going on?" her mom asked as she picked up the other receiver in another room to join the conversation.

I-35 Road Warrior

Tanyah told them what had just gone down, and then, despite her best efforts at holding back, she broke down crying on the phone.

"I'm sorry y'all. I just don't understand. Like she's blamed me for him being sick, now she's acting like I'm trying to get him possessed by the devil. How? Who does this stuff? It's ocean music! Why is this happening this way?" Tanyah cried.

"This won't last, baby," her dad said, "They'll be gone in about a week; and let them try to get any information from Taurrean himself if he can give it to them now. Otherwise they can call the hospital and fight with the nurses to see if they will give them any information. Be done. You don't need this kind of stress and you don't have to take it. You can stand up for yourself. God's not displeased with you. You have loved that boy and taken care of him better than anyone else could have. And on top of that, you've kept your household afloat and the twins are doing great. We thank God for Porsha because she has helped a lot. You have a whole village supporting you. If his family doesn't want to be a part of it, then that's their loss. They're the ones that are feeling hopeless and in despair, not us. We know the God we serve, and we're just going to keep doing that no matter what they do. Understood?"

"Yes," Tanyah choked out in response.

"Before you go back up there, I want you to read your Bible for a few minutes. After that, just say goodnight, tell your husband that you love him, and then go home and get some rest," her dad suggested.

"Okay, dad. Thanks, guys, I love you," Tanyah said as they told her that they loved her as well and ended the call.

Tanyah caught the beginning of her parents' side conversation as they were hanging up the phone. All she heard was her

That One Time My Mother-in-Law Kidnapped My Husband

dad's voice, "They're really starting to piss me off…"

***

The next week was super busy and Tanyah managed to keep her interactions with her mother-in-law to a minimum despite her growing weary of them still being there. Taurrean was improving, but still very weak and unable to walk on his own without assistance. He was more coherent most days. They were keeping him in the hospital since he was still experiencing symptoms from the GvHD.

In the middle of the week, Tanyah got a phone call from her dad. He had disturbing news and she thought she was going to lose her shit for real this time. Her mom had been in the ER but they couldn't figure out what was wrong. Things were looking pretty bad and they were now transporting her an hour away to another hospital in Waco. It was late in the evening and her dad told her not to come driving down the highway. Tanyah agreed to wait until the following day. Waco was about an hour and fifteen minutes away so it was nothing for her. She drove forty-five minutes to an hour, depending on traffic, almost every day to Dallas for months. Plus she was known to be a huge road tripper anyway.

The next day Tanyah was anxious to leave work. She'd called Taurrean and let him know that she might not make it to the hospital to see him and explained what was going on with her mom. He understood completely and reassured her that he was fine since his family was still at the hospital with him. She had the twins stay with Porsha for the night and headed down I-35 to Waco after work.

When she arrived at the hospital, she called her dad's cell to let him know that she was there. By now, she was an expert at navigating hospitals and immediately found the correct room. Tanyah hugged her dad and then went over to the hospital bed. Her mom was sitting up and talking, so that was a good sign. She gave her a hug and asked how she was feeling.

"I feel okay. I have these weird little dots all over my skin. It doesn't hurt or anything, it's just there. Barely made it to the bathroom last night," her mom said with a small laugh.

Tanyah looked at the dry erase board and read the nurse's notes. The wheels in her brain were spinning and she felt like she knew part of the problem, but couldn't pinpoint the issue. Her brain was fogged over and she was using all of the strength she had to keep from panicking. A nurse poked her head into the room to say hello and make sure that everything was okay because she'd heard more voices than usual. Tanyah was glad they were so attentive.

"So, what are they saying?" Tanyah said looking from her mom to her dad.

"They aren't really sure yet, they're still running tests and just treating all of the individual symptoms for now. But we're not worried. God's in control and we trust in *Him*," her dad said.

"Yes," her mom echoed his sentiments and added, "I'll be fine. I spoke with the Lord and *He* assured me that this is not unto death."

Taurrean told her to call him so that he could say hello to her mom, so Tanyah called and put him on speaker so that he could speak to both of her parents. It was weird since they were both asking how the other was doing in their respective hospitals. After the call, they sat and talked for a couple of hours before Tanyah's dad finally made her leave. He didn't

That One Time My Mother-in-Law Kidnapped My Husband

want her driving back home too late at night.

She headed out and filled up at the gas station before getting on the highway. She turned some music on and then all of a sudden remembered what she'd been trying to think of the whole time. She quickly dialed her dad's number and waited for him to answer.

"Hey, Tigger. You forget something?"

"No, I just remembered something."

"Hold on, let me put you on speaker because you know I won't remember what you say," her dad laughed as she heard her mom.

"Hey, Tanyah."

"Hey, mom. When the nurse comes back, tell them to check your platelet counts. That's where I remember seeing those dots and stuff that you have on your skin. Taurrean had the same thing going on and had to get platelets every month. Tell them to check for everything ASAP."

"Okay, we'll tell them and talk to you in the morning sometime," her mom replied as they said goodbye and hung up.

The drive home wasn't bad and traffic was flowing fast so Tanyah was going about seventy-five or eighty miles per hour. Her mind was racing faster than her car thinking about how her mother's symptoms were similar to her husband's. She just wanted to go home and lay in bed.

She walked up the stairs to Porsha's apartment and found that the kids were all still awake and playing. She sat and talked to her for a little while and told her about how her mom was doing. Tanyah gathered up the twins and took them back to their apartment once everyone was done running their mouths for the night. After she got them ready for bed, she called Taurrean to see if he was awake and was able to say goodnight and let him know that she'd be coming to see him after work the next day. She also let him know that their Supplemental Security Income paperwork had come in the mail earlier.

The next day was Friday, and Tanyah was more than ready for the weekend. She talked to her parents in the morning and they confirmed her previous suspicion about her mom needing platelets. They said the nurse asked if Tanyah was in nursing school or something given the way she was able to figure that out. She joked with them about maybe doing that since she'd spent the past seven months in the hospital around medical professionals speaking their language, learning new things, and picking up on the rest.

Her classes went by fast and Tanyah stayed busy with some inventory that she had to catch up on during her planning period and lunch. She wasn't really eating much because the stress was starting to get to her and she didn't have much of an appetite after breakfast time. She drank a lot of water and usually had hot tea before bed to relax, so her stomach was usually full from all of the liquids.

The twins had basketball practice after school and then they were going home with some teammates who were also twins for a birthday party and sleepover. Tanyah let them know that she would pick them up sometime before noon since they wanted to go to Waco with her to see their grandparents since her mom was still in the hospital.

Tanyah had packed a change of clothes with her since she planned to stay the night with Taurrean at the hospital and headed there straight from work. She stopped by the Starbucks in the lobby and grabbed a chai tea latte. She was hoping just

That One Time My Mother-in-Law Kidnapped My Husband

the two of them could relax and talk to each other while they watched his current favorite show, King of Queens. His family was supposed to be leaving sometime over the weekend and they'd been here long enough so she didn't expect to have any problems. Plus, she'd told him that she was coming and asked him to have them go to their hotel so that they could just hang out together.

When she got to the room Taurrean wasn't alone. She figured it was still kind of early and that they would be leaving later. They sat and talked for a little while. Tanyah didn't want to be rude and ask them to leave so she just sat through it. Eventually his mom got up to leave, but his sister said that she was staying.

"It's okay Sharee. I'm here, go ahead with your mom," Tanyah said standing up to say goodbye.

"Oh, okay because I..." Sharee began.

"No, she's staying here," Evelyn interrupted..

"I meant I'm staying the night, so y'all don't have to tonight," Tanyah clarified in case they had misunderstood.

"Well, I don't want him alone," Evelyn retorted.

"He's not alone. I'm staying the night," Tanyah said slowly so that she could get it.

"No, that's not enough. You might fall asleep and he needs something."

"With all due respect, I've literally been doing this on my own for like seven months. And he has nurses around the clock. He'll be fine," Tanyah said while she was trying to keep from putting her hands on her hips and rolling her eyes.

"Tanyah, do you mind if I just stay? We're leaving soon anyway," Sharee turned and asked.

"You know what," Tanyah started and then she stopped

herself, "Yeah. Sure. Sharee, it's fine. I actually have my blow-up bed in the trunk. I'll go down and grab it. I have to go get some more tea anyway."

Tanyah walked past Evelyn without saying a word. She wanted to shoulder check her ass on the way out, but she knew her dad would be disappointed in her, and she couldn't handle disrespecting her parents and snubbing how they raised her. Additionally, she didn't want to block her own blessings from God by being ugly. She was a little upset that Taurrean never said anything, but she just attributed it to his current state of mind and condition. He didn't need that kind of drama anyway.

That night, Sharee pretty much left them alone while she watched one of her favorite shows, Two Broke Girls. Taurrean was sleepy by the time they had gotten settled so Tanyah just watched him sleep for a while before falling asleep herself. He was stable so the nurses didn't come in as often and they were able to sleep a little longer than four hours at a time even though Tanyah still woke up every so often out of habit from watching him all this time.

The next morning, Taurrean was up and talking to Tanyah while his sister went down to the cafeteria for some breakfast. Tanyah was glad to at least have twenty to thirty minutes alone with him while she was gone. She kissed his face and prayed with him before talking about the girls and how excited they were about the upcoming basketball season. They hadn't started playing games yet, but there were some really great players on the team and it looked like their only competition would be one other middle school in their district. The other team had a few players that they previously played AAU basketball with over the summers.

Tanyah remembered the Supplemental Security Income paperwork she had in her bag and went to grab it. She explained to him that they'd gotten the approval, and it was just pending their signatures.

He hadn't received an actual full paycheck from his job since he went into the hospital back in April. He was finally able to get a little money from the disability that Tanyah made him sign up for when his employer had open enrollment the year before, but it wasn't enough to support the household, it barely supplemented all of the additional income, grants, and charity scholarships that Tanyah was able to get. That money would be running out soon. The good thing was that they were about to meet their medical deductible for the year.

One of the nurses came in and started him on his morning meds while they talked. She said he was doing much better and that the cancer didn't look to be returning. She didn't have a time frame for his release yet, but they weren't going to rush it and wanted to make sure that his body was recovering and eventually he wouldn't have any issues with the GvHD.

Tanyah sat on the edge of the bed as she explained all of the monetary stuff to him as best she could and tried to make sure it all made sense to him. She was taking care of all the paperwork and everything else in their lives, but still wanted to make sure he knew she respected him and would include him in any decisions she had to make on his behalf. She was going over the last piece of information and double-checking the accuracy of all of their answers when Evelyn walked in and saw him holding a pen.

"What's he signing?!" she yelled as though Tanyah was giving him poison.

"It's just our final SSI paperwork so that they can push it all through," Tanyah rolled her eyes and she pointed to where he needed to sign his name.

Evelyn stalked towards them, "Well, I need to see this!"

Tanyah was at her wits end as she said, "No. You actually don't."

"You're trying to trick him and steal all his money!"

"He doesn't have any damn money!" Tanyah yelled back, feeling herself unravel. She took a deep breath, turned to Taurrean, and continued, "Babe, I love you, but I'm not doing this today. Call me when they leave. I'm going to Waco to see about my mom."

"Okay," he said sleepily as the Benadryl from his meds started to kick in.

Tanyah took the paper and pen from him as he sat silently and she grabbed her bag. She kissed his cheek and walked out ready to burn the whole hospital down and she didn't even care who was in it.

She got into her car and hit I-35 once again, stopping along the way to pick the girls up from their friend's house and grabbing some food for them from McDonald's. Tanyah had lost her appetite, but knew she needed to eat, so she grabbed herself a large water and a couple of sausage burritos.

It was a quick drive to Waco and the twins were excited to go on the mini road trip. They got to the hospital room and ran to each of their grandparents to say hi. Tanyah's dad took one look at her and told her to meet him in the hallway, so that they could talk while the twins entertained her mom.

As soon as they walked out, Tanyah turned and just hugged her dad without saying a word. He put his arms around her and started praying over her. Her shoulders shook as she began to cry. Once she calmed down, they took a walk around

That One Time My Mother-in-Law Kidnapped My Husband

the hospital and she told him what was going on. Her dad listened, prayed some more, and told her to keep trusting God. He also told her that she needed to have a real conversation with Taurrean if he was able, and as politely as she could, let his family know that it was time for them to leave.

They walked back to the room to catch up on all of the stories that the twins were telling Tanyah's mom about school. Tanyah sat back and listened, realizing that she was missing so much of what was going on in their lives. They didn't seem to mind though and were very understanding. Kayla and Kaylyn were some of the sweetest girls ever, and their comical personalities were contagious. Most of the stories they told were hilarious and they had Tanyah laughing and smiling in no time.

After a few hours, her dad took the girls downstairs to the food court to grab some food while Tanyah stayed with her mom. The doctors still weren't one hundred percent sure what was going on, but they did discover that her mom had a urinary tract infection that was worse than what they normally saw in patients. She talked to her mom about the conversation that she'd had earlier with her dad and she said that she agreed with everything he said.

"I called Taurrean on his hospital room phone to talk to him," her mom added.

"You did?"

"Yes, I called to check on him and let him know that we were praying for him. But I gave him a warning as well."

Tanyah raised her eyebrows and cocked her head to the side curiously as her mom continued.

"I let him know that he needs to get his family in check and do right by you, or he's surely going to die. I've already seen it and talked to God. And it's not to frighten him or anything like that, but God isn't going to allow this to continue."

Tanyah nodded her head and sighed in agreement, "Yeah, something has to give. I told him earlier to just call me when his mom and them leave because I can't deal with that foolishness. I'm tired, not eating right, and I haven't worked out in I don't even know how long. I feel like I'm losing my mind."

Her dad and the twins returned to the room with food and they all ate dinner and chatted some more before Tanyah planned to head back. The twins wanted to hang out with some more friends and then have Tanyah pick them all up and bring them back home to spend the night at their apartment. She figured she'd indulge them and take them to church and then breakfast after.

On the way home she got a phone call.

"Tanyah," Steff said in a sing-song voice.

"Where you at?" Henry chimed in from the background.

"Hey, guys! I'm on my way back to town from seeing my mom in Waco. What the hell y'all doing out together?" Tanyah laughed through the phone.

"How is she?" Steff asked first.

"She's good. They're not totally sure what's up, but they're thinking it's just a really bad urinary tract infection that was turning septic," Tanyah updated them. She'd been texting them every week and giving them the rundown on what was going on in her drama-filled world.

"Well, we came to get drinks. You need to come join us," Henry told her.

"Aw, man. That sounds like exactly what I need, but I have the twins with me and they have plans with friends that pretty much involve me being their personal butler."

Steff and Henry laughed and groaned.

That One Time My Mother-in-Law Kidnapped My Husband

"Girl, I swear these kids be tripping me out making all these plans with no money, no car, no nothing," Steff said laughing.

"I know right. But if anything changes, I'll hit you up and come out if you're still there by the time I get back."

"Alright we'll drink something extra for you since you can't come," Steff told her.

"They don't sell wine coolers here. You know she can't hold liquor. We gotta get something else," Henry joked.

They all laughed as Tanyah ended the call and continued driving. Tanyah made it to Diane's house and went in with the twins. She must have still looked exhausted and fed up, because Diane told her to sit and just relax for a while. She gave Tanyah some tea and asked her how everything was going.

Tanyah didn't like to unburden herself on people who weren't privy to the entire situation, so she just told her that things were looking better. She explained that she had driven from Dallas this afternoon to Waco, and now back to Fort Worth trying to make sure that she split her time between her husband and her mom since they both were in the hospital. Diane was floored and didn't say anything, she just gave Tanyah a hug and a smile.

"You poor thing. You must be absolutely exhausted," Diane said after a few moments.

"I think I'm more tired mentally than physically at this point. But sleep is great because at least I don't have to think about anything," Tanyah replied.

"Well, I want to help. And I know that I can't do much, but how about you leave the twins here and I'll drop them off tomorrow after dinner?"

"Oh, no. Diane, I'm the one that's supposed to be giving you a break," Tanyah said as she smiled, feeling more blessed than she thought she should.

"Girl, please. It's nothing and you know I love those babies like my own. Besides, they're all the same size as well so we have plenty of clothes and I can wash their undergarments and stuff tonight," Diane said as she called for the kids to come into the living room.

"Hey, girls. Do you all want to stay here tonight and stay until after dinner tomorrow? You can play in the pool and we'll go to the movies and everything," Diane said, obviously bribing them with a good time.

"Yeah!" they all screamed, including her own kids.

Tanyah laughed and gave in, thanking Diane for thinking about her. She kissed the girls goodnight and then headed to her apartment which was about fifteen minutes away. She sent a text to Steff and Henry in the group chat letting them know that she'd made it back. Steff replied back saying that they'd already left the bar, but she would call Tanyah that week to catch up. Tanyah replied back, "Okay" and her phone rang. It was Henry. She connected her Bluetooth to the car before she answered.

"Hey."

"Hey, you good?" he asked.

"Yeah, the twins are staying at their friends' house so I'm kid free, which I guess isn't really that unusual these days. I feel like a dead-beat dad," Tanyah laughed.

"Well, do you want to go get a drink? I can come back out if you want."

"Naw, I just drank some tea, so I'm gonna call it a night. But next time y'all go out let me know because I'm coming dammit."

"Okay, cool. Talk to you later then."

That One Time My Mother-in-Law Kidnapped My Husband

"Nite," Tanyah said as she pressed the end call button on her steering wheel.

Eight

Shot Through the Heart

Sunday was relaxing for Tanyah. She went to her church instead of Dani's since she was actually at home in Fort Worth instead of being at the hospital in Dallas. Tanyah wasn't working with the production team that morning, but she still arrived early for the rehearsal to be able to sit in the audience alone and worship and pray by herself first. Plus, she needed to steal some more communion cups for her purse.

The team called her up onto the stage after practice and they, along with the choir, stood around her and prayed over her and for Taurrean. She was so grateful and blessed to have them and they helped provide her with some of the little things she needed here and there for the hospital. She received toiletries, bottled water, gift cards to save money on food, and natural oils and lotions for Taurrean's skin.

After church, she called him from the parking lot to see if his family had left yet and they hadn't. So, she talked to him

That One Time My Mother-in-Law Kidnapped My Husband

for a few minutes on the phone and let him know that she was going to just go back home to chill out, watch television and maybe take a short nap. She needed a break from driving, but was disappointed she still didn't have her husband to herself. He sounded a little more drowsy than he had before, but he was in the best place he could be so she didn't allow herself to be more worried or concerned than she was already feeling.

Her parents called later that afternoon to let her know that her mom was doing a lot better. The doctor still wanted to keep her in the hospital a little while longer just to make sure they kept the infection from spreading more than it already had and were able to get rid of it. Tanyah was happy to receive great news and let them know that she was taking a self-care day to just worry about herself for a change. They were glad to hear it and told her to enjoy it and have fun.

Tanyah hadn't been to the movie theater in almost a year so she decided to go check out the movie, The Girl on the Train. She usually liked to read the book before watching the movie, but there wasn't time in her schedule to read anything other than the necessary hospital or medical insurance paperwork. Plus, she really wanted to see it since the book had been a best-seller.

Besides, where else could she eat a whole box of Sour Patch Kids all by herself and drink a Mr. Pibb without having to share? She smiled happily as she put her plans into motion and headed out to have some fun by herself before the kids were scheduled to come back home from their friends' house.

Tanyah enjoyed the movie a lot and ended up grabbing a box of gummies to go so that she could give the twins some. They were excited to see her when they came home and even more excited when they got to eat some of their gummies before bed.

They wanted to talk to Taurrean for a second before going to bed so Tanyah called him on speaker phone and let them talk his ear off for about ten minutes before having them go to sleep.

She let him know that she would be heading to hospital tomorrow evening and spending the night. She assumed his family was leaving and didn't ask him this time so that she wouldn't relay how annoyed she was with them.

That next day, work went by excruciatingly slow. It seemed as though everyone needed something from her every single period of the day. She skipped lunch trying to work on a few lessons for the beginning of the week since she hadn't even thought about work over the weekend. Luckily she was very good at her job and Kinsey was the perfect complement so she never got too far behind.

By now, the twins pretty much belonged to Porsha as much as they did Tanyah and knew the routine of what to do once they arrived home from school. Tanyah still wanted to see them before she left for the hospital though, so she surprised them and picked them up from practice. She stopped at McDonald's as a treat and got them their normal order of a twenty-piece chicken nugget meal to share along with two pies. She let Porsha know that they were stopping for dinner and that Tanyah would have them shower and get all of their stuff together when they returned so that she wouldn't be waiting on them.

It wasn't too late before Tanyah got herself ready and then headed to the hospital. She'd probably arrive around 9:30 or 10 pm which would be plenty of time to catch an episode of King of Queens with him or watch something on the Amazon Firestick that she'd taken to the hospital for him. She was

That One Time My Mother-in-Law Kidnapped My Husband

still in good spirits coming off of the weekend and everyone's prayers were keeping her recharged.

She didn't even flinch or roll her eyes when she walked into the hospital room and saw his family sitting on the couch watching football. She politely said hello to everyone and then got onto the hospital bed with Taurrean and laid next to him just enjoying being there. His dad left after the game ended but of course his mom and sister stayed.

His mom was sleeping in the recliner chair and his sister was on the couch. Tanyah had the blow-up bed pulled close and touching the hospital bed and was laying halfway on each since the blow-up bed was just a twin. Taurrean had to get up a few times to use the restroom so Tanyah would help him up and basically carry him to the bathroom by allowing him to wrap his arms around her body and hold on. He was still too thin and weak to walk on his own. He hadn't even been out of the hospital bed to walk around the hospital like they used to do or even just sit up on the edge of it.

Tanyah had laughed earlier because he made his mom and sister leave the room while the nurse came in to bathe him. Tanya stood in the doorway talking to him while he and the nurse were in the huge shower area. She watched as she washed his head and the last of his hair was washed away with the shower nozzle. He seemed so relaxed and closed his eyes as the water ran over his body.

"Aht! Aht!" Tanyah playfully scolded him, "Don't be over there enjoying your little hoe bath with the nurse while I'm standing right here!"

He half-smiled as she moved down his body and washed his penis. It jumped a little and the nurse said, "Oh, I'm so sorry."

"Yeah, you see it," Taurrean said cockily and smiled at

Tanyah.

Tanyah walked over to the nurse and stood in the shower, "I got this, his ass is clowning now."

The nurse laughed and let Tanyah finish up while she changed all of the couch and bed sheets, blankets, and pillow cases. Tanyah rinsed him off and then dried him gently. She grabbed his fresh garments and hospital gown and helped him into it. By the time she was done, the bed was ready so she helped him get over to it and get comfortable. Her heart broke as she felt all of the bones in his body protruding as she held him up.

Evelyn and Sharee came back about thirty minutes after Taurrean was all settled. Tanyah appreciated the fact that they were always wanting to eat, the cafeteria was a good walk away, and neither of them was in any type of shape to make a quick trip. It allowed her to have at least a few quiet moments with him and sometimes the nursing staff as well before his loud-mouthed mother and follow-the-leader sister returned.

The nurse started a new fluid drip for Taurrean before ending her shift and let them know that it was running faster than the others so he would probably have to go to the bathroom soon. She brought in a portable toilet and put it near the bed so that Tanyah wouldn't have to help him get too far. Tanyah took the bed rail lock off but kept it raised so that he wouldn't fall out.

"He needs the rail lock on," Evelyn barked at Tanyah after the nurse left.

"He's going to be using the bathroom more often and I don't want him to be stuck or anything while I help him up. Besides, he's not going anywhere," Tanyah replied.

"Well, I think it needs to be on," Evelyn retorted.

That One Time My Mother-in-Law Kidnapped My Husband

"Babe, don't get up without me, understand?" Tanyah said to Taurrean loudly so that Evelyn could hear.

"I'm not," he replied back.

"Satisfied?" Tanyah directed at Evelyn.

"I still think it needs to be on."

Tanyah ignored her and asked Sharee if there was anything she wanted to watch on TV. She declined saying that she was getting sleepy already and got on her cellphone under the covers on the couch.

Taurrean liked to sleep with the television playing so Tanyah had King of Queens on for him and she stayed awake a little longer to watch Mike & Molly while his mom and sister fell asleep. Apparently, raising hell in Tanyah's life was such hard work that it had both of them snoring not only from being overweight, but also from all of their weeks of foolishness.

"How the hell do you sleep with all of that damn noise?" Tanyah whispered to him.

"Sometimes, I just wait until the daytime," he whispered back.

"Babe, they need to go," Tanyah said softly but sternly.

"They're leaving this week," Taurrean replied back as he yawned.

"Okay," Tanyah said and gave him a kiss as she watched him fall asleep.

Tanyah fell asleep next to him not too long afterward, still half-laying on both the blow-up bed and the hospital bed, waking up every now and then to check on him and see if he was awake or had to use the bathroom yet. Evelyn and Sharee had finally stopped calling the hogs so Tanyah was able to drift off into a dreamless sleep. Tanyah was in the middle of the rapid eye movement cycle when she heard a loud voice yelling her name and immediately woke up. She saw Taurrean standing up.

"Taurrean's up! He's not supposed to be up! He's gonna fall!" Evelyn was yelling.

The yelling startled him and he started to lose his balance. Tanyah quickly dove across both beds and into the air to try to save him from breaking a bone or something. She landed on the floor and was able to break most of his fall. Evelyn was still yelling but Tanyah wasn't paying attention.

"Are you okay, baby?" Tanyah said as a nurse ran in to help them both up from the floor.

Evelyn immediately stopped yelling when the nurse came into the room. The nurse looked at her and asked if everything was okay and she responded calmly and said that it was. Tanyah looked at her like she had five heads. She told the nurse that everything was not okay and that Evelyn was upset because Taurrean had fallen and that she was blaming Tanyah for the fall.

"Yeah, I'm sorry babe. I didn't want to wake you up. I know you've been tired," he said sheepishly.

"No, babe. You wake me no matter what. Are you sure you're okay?"

"Well, I don't have to go pee anymore," he replied.

"It's okay, we'll get it cleaned up," the nurse interjected.

Tanyah had skinned one of her elbows and both of her forearms trying to save Taurrean so she asked the nurse to help him while Tanyah cleaned up the floor and the mess that was made when they both knocked over the portable toilet. Tanyah washed herself up quickly and put on a change of clothes.

Taurrean seemed like he was still a little shaken from the fall. Luckily, he didn't have any scrapes or injuries, so the nurse

That One Time My Mother-in-Law Kidnapped My Husband

got him cleaned up in the bathroom and changed into another hospital gown and some non-slip socks. The nurse left once everything was all fixed up and told them that she'd be right outside at the nurses' station if they needed anything.

Tanyah was standing at the bottom of Taurrean's bed tucking in the bottom of the sheets when Evelyn sat up on the edge of the recliner that she was sitting in and started yelling at her.

"This is all your fault! I told you to put the lock on the bed rail!" Evelyn yelled and then stood up.

"Ma, it's okay. It was my fault," Taurrean said calmly as Tanyah just looked at her and counted to ten in her head to remain calm.

"He could have broken something! You think you're so smart! If you would've just listened then this wouldn't have happened!" Evelyn yelled even louder as she balled up her fists and then got up. She stalked towards Tanyah and got in her face.

Tanyah was stuck for a brief second between Praise is What I Do and Knuck if You Buck as Sharee got up from the couch and stood in place. Tanyah put her hands up, palms out, in a surrender position to try to de-escalate the situation. She looked her right in the eyes.

Tanyah spoke to her softly and calmly, "You need to shut yourself down, right now."

Evelyn blew up yelling and stepped even closer to her.

Tanyah blocked out everything that Evelyn was saying and kept her hands in the same visible spot as she repeated herself again, "You need to shut yourself down."

Sharee then stepped forward and began yelling at Tanyah as well, "She's a grown-ass woman, you don't tell her what to do!"

Shot Through the Heart

Evelyn and Sharee were screaming at the top of their lungs at Tanyah when several nurses came running in. Tanyah remained frozen in place with her hands raised. One of the nurses politely asked Evelyn to step outside as she continued to yell and Tanyah slowly moved to the side to make sure she didn't touch her as she stormed out and stood in the hallway. Sharee had walked back over to the couch and sat down. It appeared as though without her mother as the "hype-man" she didn't have anything else to say.

Tanyah put her hands down and tried to explain to the nurse what happened. Evelyn started yelling again. She was calling Tanyah a liar and saying that she had threatened her. Tanyah got upset and turned to Taurrean who hadn't said anything else.

"You need to tell her to leave, now," Tanyah said to him.

"I ain't going nowhere, I'm his mother!"

"And I'm his wife. Nurse, please have security come to remove her from this room if she won't leave willingly," Tanyah said calmly.

"Ma'am, please, I have to ask you to leave. This isn't good for my patient."

Tanyah looked over at Sharee, "Don't you need to go with her?"

"I texted my dad to come and get her, I'm staying."

"You sure about that? Because I don't have time for this," Tanyah told her seriously.

"Let Sharee stay, babe. Ma, just come back in the morning," Taurrean said sleepily.

"Fine! But I shouldn't have to leave! She needs to go not me!" Evelyn yelled as she stormed back into the room. Evelyn aggressively grabbed her purse and purposely swung it close to Tanyah's face pretending to only be trying to put it over her shoulder on her way out. She smacked her lips with an attitude when Tanyah didn't budge an inch.

Once Evelyn left, Tanyah walked around the hospital bed and let herself plop down onto the blow-up mattress. She was exhausted and shaking. Taurrean reached his hand through the bed rail and she turned towards him. She closed her eyes shaking her head and then began to laugh hysterically as tears ran down her face from being so upset. Small sobs escaped through the laughter and she knew at that point, she was going crazy.

"I can't believe this shit really happened," she said, still shaking her head in denial.

"I'm sorry, babe," he cautiously responded. He knew her shell was cracking and tried to calm her down, "My mom was scared. Just ignore her."

"She literally got in my face like she was going to do something to me. I'm telling you right now," and she looked over at Sharee, who'd been silent, "if something like this ever happens again, I hope you understand that I am done taking her attitude and disrespect and it won't turn out the way she thinks it will."

Tanyah looked at her elbow and forearms and kept spiraling. She started mumbling to herself, "Got my fuckin elbows missing skin and shit trying to save your ass like a damn super hero and all she did was stand there."

Taurrean started laughing for the first time in forever. Tanyah cut her eyes at him and he laughed harder.

"What the hell are you laughing about?" she said, turning her face up at him.

"Because I didn't know what you were trying to do, I just

saw you flying through the air towards me with this look on your face," he said laughing and holding his stomach.

Tanyah shook her head and started laughing as well and Sharee soon followed. All three of them were rolling as Tanyah tried to explain how it seemed like a good idea at the time, but when she hit mid-air she had second thoughts but it was too late so she had to commit to it and just prayed for the best. She leaned over and kissed him as they all began to wind down and feel how sleepy they were.

Tanyah still had to get up and drive back to Fort Worth for work in the morning. She asked him if he wanted her to take off and spend the day with him and he said yes, so she went online on her phone to go ahead and schedule the absence and told him that she'd leave in the morning to go get everything ready for the substitute and would come right back to the hospital.

She woke in the morning and wasn't as tired as she thought she would be. She hit the road and called her parents to let them know what happened.

"You need to contact the doctor and the hospital administrators about this. They need to have them removed and sent back to Georgia," her dad said.

"I know dad. I'm going to talk to them when I get back. I'm going to make sure everything is all set at work and then head back."

"They're going to be releasing me from the hospital this week and if she wants someone to put her hands on she can try me," her mom said angrily.

"It's okay, mom. I'm fine. I didn't let it get to that point," Tanyah told her.

"Call us back and let us know what the doctors and everyone

That One Time My Mother-in-Law Kidnapped My Husband

say whenever you get back then," her parents told her.

"Okay, I will," Tanyah said and pressed the end call button on her steering wheel.

She called Porsha to make sure the twins got off to school alright that morning and then told her what happened. Porsha couldn't believe what she was hearing as Tanyah gave her the rundown scene by scene. Tanyah really couldn't even believe it herself. Especially the fact that she was able to show enough restraint to not beat the hell out of Evelyn after the stunt she pulled.

They talked until Tanyah arrived at work and then she told her that she was going back up to the hospital but would be home before the kids got there. She suggested they both go to their Applebee's spot for dinner since the waiter let each of their kids eat free or half off instead of just one kid per adult meal as advertised. Porsha agreed and said that she already knew what she was going to order. They both yelled, "wonton tacos" at the same time as they laughed and then got off the phone.

Tanyah walked down the hallway to her classroom to make sure that everything was set up and ready for her substitute. She sent a quick text to Kinsey as well, so that she'd know the class was covered. Once she finished, she headed to the office to see if the principal or his secretary were in yet.

It was about 8:30 am so none of the teachers were on contract until 9 am and the school was pretty much empty with the exception of a few members of the office staff. She quickly explained what was going on and let them know that she would be out that day. Everyone understood and her principal told her to let him know if she needed anything.

Tanyah walked back to her classroom to double check that

she had all of the supplies that the students would need set out and organized and then headed back to the parking lot. She saw one of her co-workers, Mr. Gregg, on the way in and he looked at his watch and started tapping it and turning it around like it was broken. Tanyah typically never beat him into work, but the few times that she did, he always joked about the sky falling or some other natural disaster that had to be taking place since she was early. He made a joke about her going the wrong way as they walked past each other. Tanyah laughed and told him that she'd be back the next day.

Tanyah drove back to Dallas without much traffic since most of the work traffic had dissipated. She wasn't in a bad mood, she actually felt fine as she stopped at the Starbucks and grabbed a mocha Frappuccino with extra whipped cream. She planned to try and save some of the whipped cream for Taurrean, but it was almost gone by the time she exited the elevators. She kept slurping and enjoying her drink since he wouldn't know that she was going to share anyway.

One of the nurses at the main desk waved at Tanyah as she walked up and came around to talk to her.

"Hey, Mrs. Watson. Can you meet me in the conference room for a minute?"

"Sure, is everything okay?" Tanyah asked cautiously.

"Yes, of course we just needed to go over a few things with you."

Tanyah noticed Evelyn and Rick standing outside of Taurrean's room talking to another one of the nurses but she couldn't hear anything. She nodded her head in their direction out of respect since it was evident that they'd seen each other, but they both turned around and kept talking as if they didn't see her.

She followed the nurse into the conference room and noticed that several other people were there as well. Hospital security, one of the social workers that she'd spoken to, one of Taurrean's nurses, and a couple of people that she didn't recognize were all there. Tanyah turned to the social worker and smiled as she told her hello. She returned the sentiment and smiled back as one of the other doctors that attended to Taurrean was walking into the room.

"Hey, Tanyah," he spoke as he sat down.

"Hey, Dr. Owens. I did want to speak with you, but that can wait for after. What's going on? Is there an insurance issue or something I need to be aware of? The nurse said that Taurrean was okay, so…" Tanyah let her words trail off.

"No, everything is fine," the social worker now spoke up, "We just wanted to talk to you about what happened in your husband's room last night."

"Oh, yes, of course. Well, that's what I wanted to talk to you about this morning. I had to go get things ready at my job first, otherwise I would have come to you once you were on call," Tanyah directed her comments to the doctor.

She explained everything that happened and also let them know that the family was supposed to leave almost two weeks ago now, but were staying for some reason and seemed to be causing more issues rather than helping.

Everyone around the room seemed to glance at one another as though they knew something that Tanyah didn't.

The social worker spoke up, "Mrs. Watson…"

"Please, call me Tanyah."

"Yes, Tanyah, I'm sorry. The depiction of events that you just gave us is in direct contrast with what your mother-in-law and sister-in-law told us."

"Excuse me?" Tanyah asked, confused.

"Tanyah, they came to us this morning saying that you threatened both of them last night after your husband had a nasty fall and that they don't feel safe with you around."

"I'm sorry. They said what?" Tanyah asked not believing what she was hearing.

"They wanted you removed from the hospital and asked that you not be allowed in Taurrean's room."

"What?!" Tanyah said louder as she stood up ready to go fuck Taurrean's whole family up on sight.

"Mrs. Watson," the security guard said her name softly as he took a step towards the door.

Tanyah spun around towards the rest of the room, "That is an absolute lie. Where is the nurse that was on call last night? She saw what Evelyn did. She saw me holding my hands up showing that I wasn't touching her and she definitely heard everything I said, which was just me repeating myself and telling Evelyn to calm down."

"We understand, and we want to do what's best for our patient," Dr. Owens chimed in.

"I'm his wife. They can't just say I'm not allowed to see my husband. I want them gone. Now," Tanyah spoke calmly but was reeling on the inside.

"You're correct and that's what we told them. Your husband is alert so he has a say and said that he wanted both you and his family to be able to stay. We have to honor his wishes as long as he is able to speak for himself," the social worker continued.

"I'm the one that doesn't feel safe. His mother tried to fight me last night and if I would have engaged, which I didn't, his sister would have jumped in. Again, your nurse can prove that. And now they're lying about it and trying to make sure that I

That One Time My Mother-in-Law Kidnapped My Husband

can't even see my own husband? Someone needs to explain to me how this makes any sense," Tanyah pleaded her case.

"Well, we had a suggestion and wanted to see if you would be okay with everyone just having designated times so that you wouldn't be there at the same time."

"Ma'am. I apologize that I can't even remember your name right now because I'm upset. I'm done with whatever this is," Tanyah gestured around the room, "But I'm going to go see my husband right now. You and I can talk to him together if you like," Tanyah said sternly.

Tanyah walked up to the door and raised her eyebrow at the security guard. He stepped to the side and let her pass.

"Yes, of course. And it's Aubrey," the social worker responded and followed Tanyah out of the room.

"That's right. Aubrey. Thank you for reminding me. I'm sorry you have to deal with all of this," Tanyah apologized for the drama.

Tanyah walked in and owned the room like it was her classroom at school, "Give us the room and please step outside," she said with the authority of a drill sergeant to Taurrean's family as she looked each of them in the eyes one at a time. She'd learned that from her dad when she was younger and never forgot how impactful it was when he spoke to his soldiers out in public.

Evelyn started to talk, but Aubrey cut her off, "Ma'am. We don't want any more problems. Step outside."

They walked out with Evelyn still muttering to herself and Tanyah walked over to Taurrean and kissed him before asking, "What the hell happened when I left this morning?"

"I don't really remember, babe. My mom is mad because she said you tried to fight her last night and was disrespectful."

"Okay, but you were right there so you know that's not true," Tanyah said looking at him like he'd lost his mind.

"I don't know, they all said the same thing."

"You're dad wasn't even here, babe," Tanyah said, now exasperated.

"Look, they need to go home. And you need to let Aubrey know that."

"Mr. Watson, would you like for me to instruct your family to leave or did you still want them to switch off times with your wife," Aubrey asked gently.

"I just want everyone to get along," he replied weakly.

"Well, that's clearly not going to happen when your mom is lying on me and blaming me for everything that's happened to you!" Tanyah blurted out.

"Tanyah," Aubrey started.

"Fine. Aubrey please go let them know that they can be here during the day and I will come in the evenings. I'll even give them extra time until they leave so they need to be gone by 7 pm each day," Tanyah said, breathing hard.

She looked at Taurrean, "This isn't right and you know it."

Sharee came in and sat down in her customary spot on the couch while Tanyah was still standing next to Taurrean's bed. Rick came in afterwards while Evelyn stayed in the hallway yelling about how she wasn't going into the room if Tanyah was there and that it was her time to be in the room with her son now so Tanyah needed to leave.

Tanyah looked at Rick with hurt and tears in her eyes, "I don't know what your problem with me is, but allow me to remind you that I'm the one that's been here with and for Taurrean this whole time. And I've been doing it all on my own with no help from either of you what-so-ever."

That One Time My Mother-in-Law Kidnapped My Husband

"I don't know what happened last night, but we don't have a problem with you," he said.

"You've known me since I was ten years old, so you know that what she's saying happened last night absolutely did not go down like that," Tanyah took a deep breath before she continued, "It's been almost eight months, and neither one of you have ever even called me and asked if I was okay or how I was doing," Tanyah choked out as the tears flowed freely down her face now.

"I'm sorry. But he was just so skinny and small when I came this summer," Rick replied back.

"And that's my fault? Oh, wait. Breaking news, he's had cancer! If you had been here it wouldn't be such a shock. You guys have no clue what we've been going through on a day to day basis, what I've been going through being his caregiver, because all you guys do is talk to him and he has no clue what's even going on. And y'all have the audacity to question what I'm doing to take care of my family."

Tanyah wiped both of her cheeks and then kissed Taurrean as she told him she'd come back that night to see him and then left. She got in the car and screamed at the top of her lungs. Tanyah put her head on the steering wheel and let herself cry for a few minutes before trying to drive back home. She wouldn't give them the satisfaction of her dying in a car accident or something on the way. If she was going out, it would be on her own terms.

She took off down the highway and bypassed her house. She was off work and it was barely going on 11:30 am. She kept driving until she reached the hospital in Waco to see her mom. She would have plenty of time to get back into town for the girls and she had no intentions on canceling dinner with her best friend and all of the kids. Their dinners were some of the most hilarious times that the six of them had together. They were like family.

Her parents were upset about what Taurrean's family was doing. She was even more upset that Taurrean was allowing them to wreak havoc without saying anything. Her mom was ready to leave the hospital to go whoop some ass and her dad was trying to pack his things and drive back to Dallas with her. Tanyah was able to calm them both down and just talk to them for a while before having to leave so that she wouldn't hit traffic.

They all prayed together and her dad warned her to be careful driving back because the adrenaline would be wearing off soon. She made it back in record time driving at least ninety miles per hour the whole time. Porsha was home early so Tanyah walked over to her building to sit and talk to her while they waited for the kids to get home from school. The twins didn't have practice so they would be riding the bus home with Porsha's son, Brayden since they were all in the same grade. Her daughter Brandie was still in elementary so she'd be home first.

When they got to the restaurant, the kids were all chatter boxes. They twins and Brayden were excited about some new homeroom class period that they had implemented where they each got to join different interest clubs. Brayden had joined a gaming and electronics club and Kayla joined the theater club and was acting out different animals like a weirdo. They all turned to Kaylyn to see what club she'd joined and Brayden and Kayla both started laughing. Porsha and Tanyah looked at one another and then at Kaylyn as she proudly told them that she had joined the duct tape club. They all looked at each

That One Time My Mother-in-Law Kidnapped My Husband

other again and started laughing.

Tanyah didn't have much of an appetite and could only eat two of the coveted wonton tacos that she ordered, but she had a great time and needed the laughs. After they left the restaurant, Tanyah let the twins know that she would only be at the hospital for a couple of hours and then she was coming home so they could stay by themselves or go play with Brayden and Brandie until she got back. Of course they chose to play.

When Tanyah got to the hospital, she was happy to see that Taurrean was alone and she wouldn't have to fight or argue with anyone again that day. It had already been long enough and she was worn out and getting tired. She didn't want to stress him out but something had to be said.

"This needs to stop," she started.

"What do you mean?"

"What do I mean? I mean your family! What else would I mean?"

"They're just trying to help."

"Please, explain to me how that's working out for us. Explain to me the help that I've been receiving," Tanyah looked at him with daggers in her eyes.

"I don't know why you've been attacking my mom, they just came to help."

"Me? I'm the one attacking her? You gotta be fuckin kidding me, Taurrean. Your ass ain't that fuckin drugged up! You saw with your own eyes what happened and you're just gonna let them rewrite the whole story and tell you that you didn't see what we both know you did? Babe, they tried to have me removed from the hospital and not be able to even see you! You can't see that there is a problem?"

"Well, she says you're seeing someone else and stealing all

of my money and that's why you're trying to get me to sign those papers. I checked my bank account and there's only the money that they put in it."

"First of all, you don't have any fuckin money! You haven't worked since April! Do you know what month it is, Taurrean? It's November! I consolidated all of our debt together into one and I've been paying it all myself! I've been sending money to your ex for the boys! I've been paying all of our bills on my own! I've even been paying your fuckin student loan bills that have been coming! Don't you dare talk to me about "your" fuckin money when I've been supporting this family and doing everything but turn tricks in the street to make sure everything is paid! Anything I've ever had you sign was for grants and other ways for us to get free money or government assistance to help with medical and everything else. And when the hell would I have time to cheat?! You do remember that my mom is also in the hospital right? In fuckin Waco at that? I've been driving back and forth on this damn highway for weeks now trying to make sure I see you both! Does anyone fuckin care? No!" Tanyah ranted, breathing hard and now rubbing her temples trying to hold off the oncoming migraine.

"Well, you should be with your mom then," Taurrean replied with no emotion.

"She has a husband. Plus, she's in good hands. God's hands. I should be here with you. I'm your wife," Tanyah cried.

"Well, my family is here, and I want them here too just like you get to see yours."

"I love you. You know I do. I've loved you since the first time I saw you and I didn't even know your name. But we can't go on like this. I won't allow your family to treat me like I'm some random bitch off the street. I'm not coming back

That One Time My Mother-in-Law Kidnapped My Husband

up here until Sunday after church. I have to make sure things at the house are taken care of, I have paperwork to file, and I still have the twins to worry about. They've been bouncing from house to house and they deserve better. I'll talk to you on the phone throughout the day, but I need a couple of days to regroup. I love you and I'll see you later," Tanyah said as she kissed him goodnight.

"Love you," he said and kissed her back as she was leaving.

Nine

The Black Door

Tanyah took the remainder of the week off from work. She was frozen and couldn't function outside of little robotic activities like packing the twins lunches, using the bathroom and almost drowning in the shower from crying. She texted Taurrean out of habit, but couldn't bring herself to call. She tried calling the doctors to see how he was doing, but was informed that they were no longer allowed to speak with her about his care or condition per his request. Other than that she stayed in bed. She talked to Dani and promised to go to church with her on Sunday, but was doubtful about whether or not she would actually make it.

Porsha's mother in law, Vivian, had come into town to visit and the two of them stopped by to check in on Tanyah. She talked to them about what had been going on and they prayed with her, but also decided that it was time Tanyah went to see a doctor. She hadn't eaten all week and had no desire to eat or drink anything. She'd lost weight quickly and didn't care. Porsha made her some soup and she was able to have a few spoonfuls before pushing it to the side.

Depression was setting in and it was getting hard to dig herself out. She didn't want to live anymore. At this thought, she knew she had to do something and get help. Vivian and Porsha made her schedule an appointment for that Friday, and Vivian drove Tanyah to the local urgent care to see one of the doctors while Porsha said she would handle the kids after school.

Tanyah was called back almost immediately and Vivian went with her to make sure that she told the doctor everything. He was surprised she hadn't needed to come sooner after hearing all of the details surrounding her current mental state. He quickly referred her to a psychologist that could see her the next day since her practice was open on Saturdays. He told her that she would more than likely prescribe Tanyah some medication, and asked her how she felt about it. Tanyah said that she didn't care, she just wanted the noise in her head to stop. She didn't want to feel anything anymore.

The doctor advised Vivian to make sure that Tanyah wasn't left alone and to ensure that she went to see the psychologist in the morning. Tanyah gave the doctor her word as they left the office. She went and laid in bed when they returned and Vivian sat in her living room watching television. Her phone rang and she rolled over to look at the caller ID. It was her dad.

"Hey, number one," he greeted her lovingly.

"Hey, dad."

"Porsha called and told us what's going on. How are you doing?"

"I don't know dad. I just... I don't know anymore," Tanyah

The Black Door

said as tears stung her eyes.

"It's going to be okay. You're going to be okay. Your mom and I are home now if you need us."

"Thanks, dad."

"Call us tomorrow after your appointment."

"I will."

* * *

Tanyah pulled up to the psychologist's office in Southlake. It was set back off the main highway in a wooded area with a few other office buildings that surrounded it on either side. She walked to the front door that read Dr. Elizabeth Cole, suite 134. Tanyah opened the door and checked in at the front desk. The receptionist disappeared for a brief second and returned with the doctor following close on her heels.

"Hello, Mrs. Watson. Please, follow me," Dr. Cole said politely while gesturing towards the hallway behind her.

"Hi," Tanyah said quietly as she followed her down the hall.

They entered a small room that looked cozy and inviting. There was a small fireplace with paintings on the surrounding walls and a desk with a laptop computer to the left of the door. A leather reclining chair was in front of the desk with a love seat positioned opposite it. Tanyah sat down onto one of the cushions in the love seat and Dr. Cole chose the recliner.

"So, Mrs. Watson, do you mind if I call you Tanyah?"

"No, I don't mind at all."

"Perfect. You're more than welcome to call me Dr. Liz if you like."

"Thank you, I will."

"So, tell me. What brings you here? I got a little bit of

what's going on from the referring doctor, but I'd really like to hear it first-hand from you. Take your time. You're my only appointment this morning so we can spend some additional time together since this is our first meeting."

Tanyah took a deep breath and began from the beginning. She mainly looked at the floor while talking to hide the hurt in her eyes, but eventually gave up once the tears started coming. Dr. Cole handed her a tissue and a bottle of water and encouraged Tanyah to take a break if she needed it. Tanyah gauged the doctor's reactions and saw both awe and disbelief on her face as she got to the most recent events that brought her to this point.

"So, now I'm here to try to keep from going crazier than I already am," Tanyah finished.

"Well, let me first say that you are not crazy. And wow. I've never heard anything quite like this before. Just wow," Dr. Cole looked shook.

Tanyah stared at her with no emotion.

"Tell me, what have you been doing to cope? Or rather, what's been working for you?" Dr. Cole asked gently.

"I really haven't been doing anything until now. I haven't had time. I spend the majority of my time at work or in my car. I don't have time to be depressed."

"But here we are. And something has to give because it is extremely clear to me that you are suffering from some depression and we can't keep sweeping it under the rug for tomorrow. Especially, when you don't seem to be looking forward to what tomorrow may bring."

Tanyah tried to hold in the tears as her shoulders began to shake. She'd just gotten read for filth and couldn't deny any of it.

The Black Door

"I'm going to prescribe you something mild for now, and I'd like to see you again next week. Do Saturdays work well with your schedule?"

"Yes, that's fine," Tanyah said, composing herself.

"How are you sleeping? I can give you something to help you sleep as well."

"That's the one thing I can still do well without any effort. I'll be fine when it comes to sleeping."

"Okay, well I will have a prescription on standby and if you decide during the week that you need it, please call Debra up front and ask her to send it to the pharmacy for you. Again, I'm prescribing a mild antidepressant for now, just to get you started, and it will be ready for you to pick up at the pharmacy by your house as soon as you leave here."

"Thank you, Dr. Liz. I appreciate your time," Tanyah replied.

"Thank you for sharing your story with me today. If you don't have any questions, you can follow me up front and I'll be sure to have Debra put you on my schedule for next Saturday morning."

"Okay, sounds good," Tanyah said as she followed her to the front of the building.

Tanyah gave Debra the rest of her information and thanked them both again as she left. She called her parents as she got into her car to let them know that she was fine. Her dad was outside at a neighbor's house, so Tanyah filled her mom in and told her to let her dad know what was going on, so that he wouldn't worry. She headed home and stopped to pick up her prescription on the way.

The twins were running around outside when she pulled up, so she stopped to let them know that she would be home and to make sure they came in to eat. She took her medication

That One Time My Mother-in-Law Kidnapped My Husband

once she got into the house and tried to eat some soup with it, but still only got through a few spoonfuls. She made some sandwiches for the girls and put them in zip-lock bags on the table with some snacks. She'd gotten some cookies while waiting earlier so she put those out as a treat too, and then went to lay down and turned on the TV.

By the time she woke up, it was nighttime and the twins had already come in and showered. They'd eaten dinner at Porsha's house and decided to have Brayden and Brandie over to spend the night. Tanyah laughed because the four of them always made plans and hardly ever thought to include Tanyah or Porsha in their plans.

They were in the living room playing and watching the TV. Tanyah checked her phone and she had a message from Porsha that read, "Tag, you're it! Plus you need babysitters. I know you're going to the hospital and church in the morning, so just let them sleep and I'll come over and grab them all for breakfast once they get up." Tanyah quickly typed back a laughing emoji with a heart and a sincere thank you. She really had no clue how she ever would have survived without her.

The next morning, Tanyah was trying to decide what to wear. She hadn't seen Taurrean in several days, and she wanted to look nice for him and still look good for church as well. She figured that she could probably get more cooperation out of him that way. Tanyah had lost a lot of weight and it showed even though she still maintained her athletic build.

She settled on an orange, tribal print bodycon dress. It was scoop-necked and had three-quarter sleeves. The bottom fell just below her knees. Tanyah paired it with some gold hoops, a long necklace, and beige heels. She looked classy as hell with a tiny bit of sexy due to the heels, but she didn't have any

The Black Door

matching flats so she figured she'd take the risk of burning up when she walked through the church doors.

Tanyah stayed after church to talk to Dani for a little while before heading to the hospital. She wanted to check-in with her and see how she was doing mentally and physically. Tanyah didn't lie or try to smooth it all over like she normally would. If she wanted to get better she had to be honest with herself and everyone else. She told Dani that she was still struggling but that she was also seeing the psychologist again and started taking the medication that was prescribed.

Once they'd finished talking, Tanyah said her goodbyes to some of the other church members and made sure to thank them again for all of the support that they'd been giving her and Taurrean this whole time. She promised to call Dani that week and let her know how things were going as she pulled out of the parking area.

Tanyah was feeling like she was about to have an anxiety attack as she drove to the hospital. She didn't know what battle she'd be walking into and was beginning to expect the worst. She was never a glass half-empty type of person, so these feelings of dread were new. She'd just come from church and it seemed as though everything she'd gained was fading the closer she got.

In her mind, Tanyah was clutching for dear life and holding on to the proverbial full armor of God as she walked down the hospital corridor. She stopped at one of her and Taurrean's former chill spots and sat for a second. She was reminded of something that her dad always told her, "If you're gonna pray about it, then don't worry. And if you're gonna worry about it, then don't pray."

Tanyah decided to sit and pray. She practically begged God

That One Time My Mother-in-Law Kidnapped My Husband

for peace and comfort. She prayed earnestly that he would cover her and protect her from any harm that she might be walking into. Especially in heels. She didn't get up or move until she felt calm and collected.

She walked with her head high to his hospital room, stopping by the nurses station to say hello to the ones on staff for the day. They all said hello back and complimented her on the dress she was wearing. Tanyah entered Taurrean's room with a smile and maintained the smile even though his sister was there. She gave him a kiss and said, "Hey." She was going to talk to him come hell or high water and nothing was going to ruin that. She was his wife and nothing else mattered.

"Hey, Sharee. Can you excuse us, please? I'd like to have a conversation with Taurrean alone."

"No," she replied back nastily.

"Excuse me?" Tanyah asked, not sure she'd heard her correctly.

"I'm not going anywhere. He doesn't need to be alone with you," Sharee spat back in an angry tone.

"I'm his wife, I can talk to him alone, thank you," Tanyah said looking over at Taurrean with a raised eyebrow.

"Well, I'm his sister!" Sharee yelled.

Tanyah remained calm and smiled at her before turning to Taurrean, "Do you see what's happening here? What you're allowing to happen?"

"They're just trying to look out for me," he said defiantly.

Tanyah glanced at Sharee out of the corner of her eye and saw that she was recording their conversation on her cell phone. Tanyah vowed to remain sane and not give her any ammunition for whatever it was that she was trying to accomplish.

The Black Door

"Babe, I'm your wife. You do remember that don't you?" Tanyah asked as he remained silent. She gave him a few seconds and then continued, "What exactly is it that you want? Because this is becoming unbearable and extremely stressful for me. Answer me this, do you really think God is going to bless us with things the way they are?"

"I don't know," he replied without any emotion.

"Yes, you do know. There's no way that you don't," Tanyah replied, feeling herself become irritated and hurt at his aloof answers. Tanyah moved closer to him and grabbed his hand as tears began to run down her face, "I'm. Your. Wife. Or does that not matter to you? Don't you even want to be married anymore?"

"I don't know anymore. No, I don't think I do."

Tanyah's heart stopped. She closed her eyes as the mascara ran into her tear ducts and stung the fuck out of her already red-rimmed sockets. She couldn't breathe. Tanyah managed to get out a weak "Okay, I'll just talk to you later" before she kissed him on the lips and walked out of the hospital room clutching her chest. She felt like she was having a heart attack. Tanyah took off her heels and waved off the nurses trying to figure out what was wrong with her as she stumbled her way past them to the parking garage.

She sat in the car crying and screaming at the top of her lungs for about fifteen minutes until her throat was raw and she could no longer hear herself. The tears kept coming and wouldn't stop. Tanyah was a wreck. She was angry and furious for only a brief moment and then she felt desperate. She started to fire off a text to Taurrean's dad, but then decided to just call. He didn't answer so she left a distraught voicemail begging him to take his family back to Georgia so that she and Taurrean could fix whatever was going on with him because them being here was just making things worse. She let him know that Taurrean was saying that he didn't know if he wanted to be married anymore and they had to help her fix this.

Tanyah waited around thirty minutes for a call back, while also attempting to reach Rick again with no luck. She took a deep breath to steady herself and drove back home like a robot. She'd driven that highway so many times that everything from the signs to the construction bumps was ingrained in her head. Her body went through the mechanics to get her home, but she had no clue how she'd arrived when she opened her front door. She walked to the living room and let her purse fall to the hardwood floor. She followed with a loud thud.

* * *

Tanyah was stirred back to consciousness by her phone ringing. It had been about twenty minutes since she passed out and she was disoriented trying to remember where she was. She clicked accept on the phone call, but didn't put it up to her ear as she walked slowly towards her bedroom. She heard someone saying, "Hello? Tanyah, are you there?" and remembered that she was holding the phone in her hand.

"Hello?" Tanyah said with a strained voice and not looking at the call screen to see who it was that had called.

"What's going on, Tanyah? What's wrong?" her dad asked with concern.

Tanyah was exhausted and didn't shed a single tear as she recanted what happened earlier at the hospital. She stared at the black screen on her television with no emotion and barely blinking.

The Black Door

"Tigger?"

"Yeah?" she answered.

"I know where you're at baby. I've been there. You can't give up or give in to that darkness," he encouraged her as she remained silent. He talked to her about the heartache he experienced in his young adult years and the family trauma that had led him down that path.

"Tanyah, I know it feels like there's no way out. I know you feel helpless. But whatever you do, don't go through that black door. You know what I'm talking about and I need you to promise me."

Tanyah spoke up, "I won't dad. I promise." She began to cry again softly.

"I know, baby girl," her dad consoled her over the phone, "I'm so sorry this is happening. I don't know what God has planned, but you have to trust *Him*. You have to trust *Him*, babe."

"I do, dad. I just don't know what else to do. I have nothing left to give."

"You don't have to do or give anything else. Just let God take care of it. Let Taurrean's family take care of him for now since they're here. That's what they want to do and what he wants them to do. Right now, you need to take care of yourself. You are no good to those girls like this."

"Okay, dad."

"Alright. Don't make us have to come up there. Clear as day?"

"Yes, dad. I understand. I love you."

"Love you more," he told her as they hung up.

Tanyah tried calling and texting Taurrean but he wouldn't answer his phone. When she called the hospital room, either

That One Time My Mother-in-Law Kidnapped My Husband

his mom or sister would pick up and when she asked for them to put Taurrean on the phone they would hang up on her. She didn't know what else to do, because going back up to the hospital was not an option. She would end up in jail if she did.

After she'd stopped calling for the day, she got a text from his sister saying that they wanted to use Taurrean and Tanyah's other car and requested that she have the keys waiting for them along with a check she'd told him that they finally got and his sister had overheard the conversation. To avoid the drama, Tanyah put it all outside on the doorstep. She really hoped someone would come by and just steal both.

Ten

When Everything's Made to be Broken

Tanyah still wasn't eating much that week and was mainly going through the motions at work now. Kinsey was picking up most of the slack, and Tanyah was just another warm body in the classroom. The students could tell something wasn't right and were extra helpful and worked ten times harder than usual trying in their own way to make things better.

She'd just thrown herself back into it and was drowning herself in project after project. Anything to stay busy. The twins still had basketball practice, so Tanyah went directly from work to their practices that week and stayed the whole time just to get out of the house.

Tanyah walked outside of the gym. She'd gotten a notification on her phone saying that the cell phone bill was past due. She smacked herself on her forehead as she remembered that

That One Time My Mother-in-Law Kidnapped My Husband

the cell phone bill was the one bill she hadn't transferred into her name since Taurrean already had the bill on autopay from his account. He'd just combined her account with his and then added the twins to the plan.

Apparently, the bank account was no longer connected for payment, and for whatever reason, the phone company actually had a problem with her trying to pay the bill without all of the information. Tanyah was frustrated and since Taurrean wasn't speaking to her or couldn't, she asked to have her and the twins' phone lines separated to another account that she would be in charge of and could pay. The representative said that Tanyah would still need to get Taurrean to call in to approve it. She tried to explain what was going on, but they wouldn't budge. She was able to get an extension on the due date but wasn't sure what to do.

Tanyah texted and called Taurrean and his family again with no answer, letting them know the circumstances and hoping for some type of reply or resolution. She called her parents and told them what the problem was in hopes that maybe his parents would speak to them instead and she could get everything done that way. They weren't able to get through, but when Tanyah called back, Taurrean answered.

"Why aren't you answering my calls?" Tanyah asked furiously.

"I couldn't find my phone," he said, sounding exhausted.

"Yeah, well, news flash, your mom or sister probably took it until you asked for it because I've been calling your room and they've been hanging up on me!" she shot back at him and he remained silent.

"Look," she began more calmly, the phone bill isn't being paid anymore for some reason and I need access to the phone

When Everything's Made to be Broken

account to pay it otherwise I have to separate the accounts to pay it. But either way, I have to call you on the phone for them to do it."

"He doesn't need you to pay anything, you just worry about yourself!" Tanyah heard Evelyn yell in the background.

She was pissed that he had her on speaker phone, but the way he sounded had her convinced that his mom probably handed the phone to him like that when he answered.

"Babe, don't hang up. I'm going to call the actual store so that we can get this done quickly and don't have to wait long for customer service."

Tanyah merged their call with T-Mobile and somehow Taurrean was able to give all of the information to the manager so that they could separate the cell phone accounts and all maintain the same phone numbers. After the process, Tanyah asked him to stay on the phone so that they could talk but she heard Sharee in the background this time yelling about him being tired. The phone went dead before she could say goodbye and tell him that she loved him.

On Wednesday, Tanyah sat at her desk during her free period reading a novel about vampires for fun and to take her mind off of everything that was going on in her life. She was turning the page when her cell phone rang.

"Hello?" she answered while looking at the screen and not recognizing the phone number.

"Hey, Tanyah. It's Helen from the main office."

"Oh, hey, Helen. What's up?" Tanyah greeted her nicely.

Helen was the property manager of the apartment complex that Tanyah lived in and they talked every so often in passing. She mainly saw the twins outside every day and they talked to her more. They also brought her cupcakes periodically when

That One Time My Mother-in-Law Kidnapped My Husband

Tanyah had extra.

"Nothing, much really. I was just calling to check in because you didn't let me know that your husband was getting out of the hospital today and he's here in the office with his family because they don't have a key to get in. His mom or maybe his sister I guess said that they were all leaving somewhere," Helen replied.

"What? What do you mean he's in your office? He's not supposed to be out of the hospital. How is he even there?" Tanyah asked frantically.

"Well, yeah he doesn't look too good and he's barely able to hold himself up on the walker he's using," Helen said now sounding concerned.

"Stall them and don't give them a key. I'm leaving now and can be there in like fifteen minutes," Tanyah said as she ran full speed out of the school building to her car.

"I'll stall as much as I can, but his name is on the lease and he has his ID with him, so I have to give him a key."

"Okay, just do what you can. I'm on my way!" Tanyah said as she hung up the phone and called the main office of her school to let them know that she had an emergency with her husband and had already left the building.

Tanyah flew down the road and sped up over the railroad tracks barely missing the cross rails as they were coming down for the usual afternoon train. She wasn't going to let anything keep her from getting home in record time. She sped through all of the yellow lights that she seemed to be getting and drove like she was on a race track to get to the apartment gates. She drove around to the back of her apartment since that was quicker and hopped out of the car. She ran up the small hill to her door and Evelyn was coming out of their apartment.

When Everything's Made to be Broken

"You stupid ass bitch!" Evelyn immediately yelled at Tanyah when she saw her.

Tanyah stared at her in such disbelief and confusion that she couldn't even yell back when she spoke to her, "Huh? What are you even doing here? And why is Taurrean not in the hospital? Where is he?"

Tanyah stopped listening to her yelling and calling her everything but her name. She heard the word "hoe" as Evelyn walked down the sidewalk and she turned the doorknob to get into her apartment. It was locked, so Tanyah used her keys to unlock it. It still wouldn't open and she realized that someone was inside and had the deadbolt on the door. Tanyah quickly called the apartment manager and told her to bring the community police officer that was on-call with her. Tanyah banged on the door and yelled for whoever was in there to open it.

Sharee came to the door and yelled back that she wasn't opening the door and then started yelling for Tanyah not to touch her.

Tanyah yelled through the door, "What the hell are you talking about?! I'm not even in the house with you! But I'll tell you this, if I have to kick this door down and pay for the repairs, I can guarantee you that I will be touching you! Now open up my damn door!"

Sharee opened the door and then ran to the kitchen. She immediately started yelling at Tanyah. Tanyah could tell that she had her phone out recording the audio of their interaction.

"Stay away from me! Don't you fuckin touch me!" Sharee yelled from more than ten feet away.

Tanyah rolled her eyes at her as she responded dryly, "I'm not even near you, you fuckin retard. Get the hell out of my

That One Time My Mother-in-Law Kidnapped My Husband

house before I remove you myself. And the police are on their way."

Tanyah didn't wait for her to respond as she rushed to her room and saw Taurrean sitting on the edge of the bed looking at a paper.

"Babe? What are you doing? What's going on? Why are you out of the hospital?" Tanyah asked him softly.

Just then his phone rang and she watched as he slowly answered it and seemed to be slurring his words. All she heard was a series of "uh, huh" and "yeses" before he ended the call.

"Babe," she said a little more forcibly, "What is going on?"

"I'm going to Georgia," he said slowly, still slurring his speech.

"What do you mean you're going to Georgia?! You're supposed to be in the hospital!"

"I'm going... Going to a better hospital," he said as his words were now breaking up.

"A better hospital? Then your ass should be going to Houston then because that's where the best hospital for cancer is right now!" Tanyah said louder and got frustrated.

She could tell that he was out of it and it didn't seem like he really knew everything that was going on. Tanyah breathed in and out slowly and then looked up at the ceiling. She looked around the room and then out into the living room.

"Where is all of our stuff?" Tanyah asked, realizing that random shit was missing.

"I need my stuff."

"To go to a hospital? What stuff? All of your clothes that don't even fit? A fuckin blender? Are you gonna make smoothies in the hospital now? This doesn't even make sense! YOU don't even make sense!"

"Tanyah? Are you in there?" Helen called from the front door.

"I'm back here in the room, Helen!" Tanyah yelled back, unable to control herself as she walked out to meet her.

There were two officers with her and Tanyah nodded in their direction as they nodded back and each acknowledged her with a "Ma'am."

"Hey, I'm keeping them out but they're wanting him to come out and starting to get irate," Helen popped her head around the corner, "Mr. Watson, your family is asking for you."

"Taurrean, are you sure you want to do this?" Tanyah pleaded with him as she walked back to the room.

He was struggling to get up and couldn't seem to balance on the walker. Tanyah started to tear up as she went to help him and hold him up while he barely shuffled.

"I'm gonna call you. I'm gonna call you when I get off the plane," he mumbled into her shoulder as she helped him out of the house.

Evelyn came up the sidewalk and spat out, "I got him!" and yanked the walker away from Tanyah, almost knocking Taurrean over. Tanyah balanced him while Evelyn took over and Taurrean whispered weakly, "I'm gonna call you when I get off the plane."

Tanyah walked back into the apartment and sat on her couch. Helen started talking and then stopped when she realized that Tanyah wasn't listening.

"Tanyah?"

She looked up at her with tears.

"The family said that they're moving him to Georgia and they want access to your garage storage so that they can get his stuff. They'll be coming back for it later though, they're

That One Time My Mother-in-Law Kidnapped My Husband

leaving for now. They asked that the garage be left unlocked. I have to get your permission as well."

"It's fine. I don't care, they can take whatever they want. That shit doesn't matter to me," Tanyah said, still staring straight ahead.

"Okay. I'm sorry, girl. Call me if you need anything," Helen said as she squeezed Tanyah's shoulder and then left.

"Ma'am? Is there someone we can call or anything we can do for you before we leave?" one of the officers asked gently.

"My mother-in-law basically just kidnapped my husband from the hospital and is now taking him to Georgia. You literally saw the medical state that he was in. Can you do something about that?" Tanyah asked sarcastically, looking from one to the other.

"Unfortunately, no, we can't. We're sorry," the other one replied for both of them.

"Of course. Everyone is always sorry."

The officer handed her both of their business cards and told her to call them if the family came back and was causing any problems.

"Sure. Thanks," Tanyah replied as she leaned back on the couch.

She heard the door close and just stared at it. She finally picked up her cell phone and called her parents.

"They took him, dad," Tanyah cried into the phone, "They just came and took him and now he's gone. They're taking all of his stuff and moving it to Georgia like he's never coming back."

"I know. His dad called us. They're hurt and they're grasping at straws on what to do. They don't know what they're doing. Your mom and I tried talking to them, but there's no reasoning with them. Let them have whatever they want, don't fight over anything. You know that God always blesses us and we'll replace it. Don't worry. Stay strong, and keep concentrating on getting yourself better. Don't let this be a setback."

"Okay, dad."

"We love you. Everything is going to be okay. Let God take care of them," her mom chimed in.

"I love y'all too."

Tanyah sat on her couch in the same spot for hours. Eventually, the twins came home and she was still sitting there. Taurrean never called. She tried to call him, but his phone just went straight to voicemail every time. She tried texting him, but they were all left unread. She told the girls that Taurrean had gone to a different hospital in Georgia with his family. They had a lot of questions that she couldn't answer. She couldn't explain why they didn't get to see him before he left.

As Tanyah walked to her car Saturday morning, she noticed that something was off. She got into the car and just sat with this odd contemplative look on her face for a few minutes.

"Wait. I know the fuck…" Tanyah whispered out loud to herself and hopped out of the car.

Tanyah walked up and down the parking lot and then ran over to her garage. Her other car was missing. She walked around the entire apartment complex just to be sure before going to the manager's office. Tanyah saw Helen and asked her if any vehicles had been towed. Helen looked alarmed as she told her that no cars had been towed in awhile. She asked Tanyah for her car information. Tanyah began describing the Ford Expedition and Helen stopped her before she got to the license plate.

"Tanyah, you're husband's family took that car the day they

That One Time My Mother-in-Law Kidnapped My Husband

came here. I just assumed that you knew. I think some of his cousins or someone came back and got it, along with some more stuff out of your garage. They had asked me to escort them along with his dad."

"They stole my fuckin car?!"

Tanyah's appointment with Dr. Liz that morning wasn't helpful. She hadn't really wanted to talk anymore, but she did want to get better so she forced herself to go and told her as much. But when Tanyah started telling Dr. Liz everything that had occurred that week, Tanyah got upset. She wasn't upset at that moment because of what was happening to her, she was upset because the doctor was genuinely shocked, confused, and literally said that she couldn't believe what she was hearing.

How was Tanyah supposed to get help and get better if her story and life was so outlandish that even a medical professional who was trained in human behavior and the mind had absolutely nothing to say? Tanyah left that day and told the receptionist that she would call to make the follow up appointment later after she checked her schedule, but she had no intentions of calling that office again.

Over the next couple of weeks, Tanyah tried relentlessly to contact Taurrean. His phone still went directly to voicemail and her texts were going unanswered. She tried calling his family but no one would ever pick up or message her back. She foolishly even tried sending a letter to him directly in the mail to his parent's house in case he was out of the hospital and staying there with them. She didn't receive a phone call or anything back. She hadn't even been receiving mail lately for some reason.

Tanyah called the hospital in Dallas to speak to his doctor. Dr. Campbell apologized for everything that had happened to them and told her that she couldn't really give her much information. Dr. Campbell was sad for her and tried to reassure her that she would do whatever she could on her end to monitor his care in Georgia and contact her with any information that she was allowed to share. As of yet, no one had contacted her about him.

Tanyah described to her how he'd been acting and how he looked the day he left. She asked how he was even able to leave the hospital. Dr. Campbell informed her that there wasn't anything she could do and that he'd been discharged against medical advice and that, while it would be noted with the insurance company, it wouldn't affect their premiums or coverage.

Tanyah couldn't seem to find where she put any of their paperwork and hospital information. She kept it all in a bright yellow folder so that Taurrean could easily find it, but Tanyah must have misplaced it with all of the mess and drama going on. She finally found some old paperwork in a random dresser drawer and was able to get the number for the doctor that he'd initially been seeing in Georgia when he was first diagnosed with cancer. She called the office and was able to speak to one of the staff members. She informed Tanyah that he was no longer a patient with that doctor or with the hospital and that they couldn't give her any other information.

She was already concerned with the lack of communication, but now she was worried. She called the local Georgia police station that would be in charge of the county where his parents lived and explained her situation. They said that she couldn't file a police report since no crime had been committed, so she asked them to conduct a welfare check. They told her that they would and that they would call her back with their findings.

That One Time My Mother-in-Law Kidnapped My Husband

Tanyah waited a day and then called them back. All they said was that no one would answer the door to the home and that they couldn't make them. Tanyah begged them to try again and to have the officer call her when he arrived at the home. The department sent an officer out and he called saying that he was officer Reynolds and that he was pulling up to the home.

Tanyah heard him get out of his car and walk up to the door. She heard him ring the doorbell and then follow up with the customary knocks as well.

"There are cars in the driveway so it appears as though someone is home, ma'am. But no one is answering the door," officer Reynolds told her.

"Can you maybe try announcing yourself and see if that works?"

"Sure," he said as he moved the phone from near his mouth so that he wouldn't be yelling in her ear. He rang the doorbell again and knocked louder as he said, "This is officer Reynolds with the Jonesboro Police Department. I'm here to conduct a welfare check on Taurrean Watson."

He waited for a few moments and then knocked again.

"I'm sorry. If anyone is here, and I suspect that they are, no one is answering. We can't kick the door down."

"Okay, thank you for trying," Tanyah said.

Eleven

Tear-Stained Letters

Tanyah had a yellow spiral notebook that she always kept by her bed in case she needed to write something down while she was on the phone. She tore out the first couple of pages that had been written on and started writing short notes or letters to Taurrean every few days or so, knowing that the only way he would ever see them would be when he came home or if she drove to Georgia, found him, and read them to him. Thanksgiving flew by without a word from him and Tanyah went back to work; and, it was business as usual.

Wednesday, 11-30-16

Today at lunch, this kid walked by me with green snot coming out of his nose and sitting all over the top of his lip. As he walked by me, he started licking it off the top of his lip. I immediately started dry-heaving and thought I was going to lose my lunch that I just ate. The only thing that kept me from barfing was one of my students that saw the whole thing and was laughing so hard at me that he was red in his face. I can never unsee what I just saw. I hope I don't have bad dreams.

Love, Tan.

Tanyah's birthday would be here in a week and she hadn't spoken to her husband at all. Never in a million years would she have considered the fact that she'd be spending her thirty-fourth birthday without him there to take her out to dinner or at least do something small and romantic at home or even in the hospital. He would have tried to make that happen. All she wanted right now though was a phone call. She still texted his phone every day but had stopped calling since it always went straight to his voicemail and the mailbox was full now so she couldn't leave any more messages.

Thursday, 12-1-16

I mailed you a letter and some mail that the mail people keep forgetting to forward. It's mostly junk mail, but I figure it may be fun to read. I requested a signature so I would at least know that you got it since you didn't reply to the last one. The mail carrier said no one was there so they left a post office notice.

Love, Tan.

Tanyah wanted to drop everything and go to him, but she couldn't leave just yet. Her school would be out in a few weeks, so she planned to leave the twins with her parents and make the drive to Georgia during the Christmas break so she wouldn't have to rush back. Her mom and her mom's best friend, Rhonda, had other plans for her though. Rhonda's daughter, Dawn, and some of her cousins were all going to New Orleans that weekend for a girls' trip.

Dawn and Tanyah had grown up together since their parents were all best friends in the military so they were more like sisters than friends. Plus, Tanyah had gotten popped with a ruler many times by Rhonda when she was younger for being a rascal all the time so it was obvious their families were close.

Tanyah had never been to New Orleans, and because of everything that was going on, they had talked to Dawn and all decided that Tanyah needed to get out and just enjoy herself. Her birthday was coming up and one of the cousin's birthday was a couple of days before Tanyah's so they would be celebrating together. She was nervous and excited and couldn't wait to tell Taurrean about it.

Friday, 12-2-16

Decided to go on a girls' trip this weekend. Well, actually I was coerced into going and they bought my flight before I could say no, but I'm excited about going now. We're going to New Orleans and since I've never been they're paying for everything. Rhonda and my mom paid for my flight, and Dawn got our hotel. She was on the Houston news as her first detective TV debut last night. Her and her partner caught a serial rapist that had been torturing women in Houston since like before this summer. She was so pretty and all take-charge and stuff! I think I screamed during the whole thing so I had to watch it twice. Anyway, I can't wait to eat some of those powdered sugar, fried donut things that they have in New Orleans. I'll eat an extra one for you. Love, Tan.

The entire girls' weekend was wild and a lot of fun. Tanyah laughed and smiled the whole trip and didn't let what was going on in her life stop her from having a great time. Even when a few guys approached her wanting her phone number, she'd just nonchalantly say, "Sorry, guys, I'm married." Of course, for whatever reason, every man thinks that's an invitation to ask where said husband is if they don't see him, so her default response was, "My husband isn't here because he's been battling cancer all year and his mom just kidnapped him from the hospital."

Tanyah always had dark humor and loved getting a reaction out of people. After those exchanges, she just went back to jumping around in the air and pretending to know how to dance.

Monday, 12-5-16

OMG! This weekend was so freakin cool! So, on Friday, my flight to New Orleans left at like 7:30 pm. My aunt Sandy sent me drink coupons to get a drink on the plane so I tried a vodka cranberry. It was so yummy! It had me tipsy though because when I got off the plane and was picking up my bag I got the zippers all stuck in my ripped jeans. LOL! It was funny. After we took my stuff to the hotel, we went out to Bourbon Street. I had a drink called the Green Grenade and a Fireball shot. We went into like every club and just danced and jumped around. They said that after a while though, they kept yelling at me because I started picking up all of the trash and stuff on the floor in the club. Hahaha! I guess I like to clean up when I'm drunk... I had a huge headache in the morning. I thought it was gonna like explode or something. We had some breakfast at this super cool place and they had melted butter in a little pour thing to put on your pancakes. It gave me so much life! All I could think about was wishing you were there so you could have some butter too. I ate so much I had to take a nap! That night we went back out so I tried a Hurricane drink. It didn't taste strong, but after like thirty minutes I was gone. The lights in the club had me thinking I was in a war zone or something, but other than that I was a dance machine! Sunday, we just ate at a bunch of different places and walked around the mall and I played the penny machine at the casino and won ten bucks. I had a super fun time. Can't wait until you and I can go together. The mall had this huge Christmas tree up. The base was like ten feet wide!

Love, Tan.

Tanyah found that writing her notes to Taurrean seemed to work a little better than the therapy sessions that she'd tried. She still hadn't been completely transparent with him though even in her writing. Sometimes she wanted to tell him that she missed him more than anything in the world, other times she wanted to curse him out like a sailor. More often than not she just wanted to write little prayers for him and a few lame jokes that she'd heard over the years that still made her laugh out loud. But when her birthday came and she still hadn't heard from him or gotten a returned text or call, she broke down crying.

She got a Facebook notification before going to bed saying that he'd unfriended her and changed his marital status to single. He didn't even know how to use Facebook. She was the one who'd set up his account. Tanyah was furious. The tears burned winding trails down her face, and that sent her over the edge even more. Tears stained the paper and the pen scratched through the page leaving holes as she wrote heavily, silently begging him in her mind to come back to her. She threw the notebook at the wall and paced back and forth in her room. She was breathing hard and trying her best to get it under control.

Tuesday, 12-6-16

Today is my birthday. You still haven't called. I wonder if you even remembered. I've been crying all morning thinking about it. I've been calling, texting, and even emailing you since you left. Every day. I even sent you letters in the postal mail and no one has gone to the post office to pick them up. You changed your Facebook relationship status from married to single and deleted me. Today

That One Time My Mother-in-Law Kidnapped My Husband

won't be a nice letter. I wish I could punch you in your face. Until tomorrow then...

Heartbroken, Tan.

Tanyah went through the motions at work as it was becoming the usual for her. She felt a range of emotions that came in sporadic waves of intensity. She was biding her time until Christmas break which was only one more week away. Tanyah could hardly wait to go to Georgia, find her husband, and wring his neck for putting her through all of this nonsense. If he wasn't in the hospital when she got there, he would be by the time she got done with him and dragged him back to Texas. She chuckled to herself and shed a tear thinking about being able to finally kick his butt for real once he was fully healed and back home.

Wednesday, 12-7-16

I don't want to talk to you today. I'm still upset that you didn't call for my birthday. Or at all, period. I love you, but I still want to punch you.

Love, Tan.

Tanyah was excited about Thursday when she woke up. It was game day for the twins and she loved being able to go watch them play. She was never a basketball fan, but her kids had converted her to the "Ball is Life" crew and she was enjoying it a lot. Tanyah was mainly into cross country and track and field since she had competed in those sports her whole life.

Her parents were usually at every game, but they had appointments and some other errands to run so they couldn't make it this week. The twins played great, as they always did. Kayla scored double digit points and Kaylyn had a few points and some huge defensive plays in the winning game. Their team was a powerhouse and everyone was looking forward to all of the girls continuing on together in high school. Some of the high school coaches were already talking about the twins and their teammates in other conversations within the school district.

Tanyah ordered the twins some pizza while they were finishing up in the locker room and went home to catch the delivery person since they said that they were catching a ride home with a friend and her parents who also lived in their apartment complex and had come to the game. They were staying to watch the end of her little brother's game in the other gym so it wouldn't be long before they got home.

The boys' team had won their game as well, so the twins were on ten when they arrived. They had the hilarious habit of always talking a mile a minute to Tanyah at the exact same time. She just laughed as she tried to keep up with what they were saying happened during the game. A few of the boys were already around six feet tall and were dunking at the end of the game. The twins were reenacting the whole thing and jumping around the house.

They cleaned up the kitchen and Tanyah made sure the twins showered and had all of their equipment in the washing machine before bed. She'd get up early in the morning and switch it all over in case they needed sports bras or practice clothes for athletics. Their coach was a winner and she didn't believe in days off after a game. They would still be doing something in class, just not with as much intensity as game play. The three of them went to bed happily exhausted and glad that it was almost the weekend.

Tanyah was in a deep slumber, when she woke up in a panic. Her chest was being clenched tight and she couldn't seem to

That One Time My Mother-in-Law Kidnapped My Husband

catch her breath. Was this what a real heart attack felt like? Was it an anxiety attack? She was sweating like she'd had a nightmare, but couldn't remember and tried to slow her breathing. She was feeling dizzy and lightheaded as she tried to look for her phone in the dark, but couldn't move. And then it all stopped.

She was finally able to concentrate and grabbed her phone. The time read 1:10 am. Tanyah jumped out of bed and turned on her bedroom light, running to the bathroom. She splashed water on her face and looked in the mirror trying to see if anything was visibly wrong with her. She lifted her shirt and examined her chest as if she had x-ray vision.

"What in the entire fuck just happened?" Tanyah whispered to herself out loud, as she lowered her shirt.

Tanyah climbed back in bed, but turned on one of her lamps in the corner of the room after turning off the main lights. She closed her eyes and took a deep breath before laying back on her pillows. She smiled and had no clue why; a wave of unexplained love and peace washed over her. She felt like God was telling her that everything was okay, and she fell back asleep.

Tanyah woke up early and was surprisingly rested. She switched the clothes in the washer over to the dryer and made the girls a quick, hot breakfast so that they wouldn't have to make cereal. She even made their lunches for them and wrote little "I love you" notes to both of them and hid them in their lunchboxes. Tanyah had some pep in her step and she was grateful. She'd been in the doldrums the past few weeks and hadn't seen a way out.

She got the twins off to school and then headed to work herself. She called her parents on the way to check in and let them know about the basketball game the night before.

"Hey, mom," Tanyah said as her mom answered the phone.

"Good morning. Your dad already left to go to his other appointment. What's up?"

"Nothing much, I was just calling to fill you guys in about the game last night."

"Oh, yeah. The twins called us already while they were on the bus," her mom said laughing.

"They called y'all that early?" Tanyah laughed as well.

"Yes, they did. Your dad was still here. We just got off the phone with them a few minutes before you called and your dad left after."

"Oh, okay. Well, it sounds like you already got the scoop then, so all I have to say is that they played really well," Tanyah laughed again.

"Yep, they told us every little detail. It was like we were there. We're coming next week though. They were asking where we were at," her mom said with a chuckle, "So, how are you doing?"

"You know what? The weirdest thing happened last night. I can't really explain it," Tanyah refrained from going into details so that she wouldn't cause any panic, "But, I feel different this morning."

"What do you mean?" her mom asked curiously.

"I feel like something left me, almost like a weight was lifted off of me. I don't know what it is exactly. It's like a weird calmness," she tried to explain.

"The peace of God," her mom stated plainly.

"Yes! That has to be it, because I have no words for it," Tanyah agreed.

The rest of the day went by pretty fast and she got a

notification on her phone that the mail she'd sent to Georgia weeks ago had finally been picked up from the post office. She was feeling hopeful. The twins called and told her that they were staying after school for a faculty vs. students volleyball game. Tanyah had some time to herself, so she decided to write Taurrean another letter in her notebook.

Friday, 12-9-16

I woke up happy today. I'm still sad, hurt, and I miss you a lot, but I feel like a weight has been lifted from me. The pain isn't crippling me anymore. I can smile and laugh without having to force back tears. I love you and I wish you were here. I won't stop praying for your health or our marriage; but, I can't make you love me or honor our commitment to God and each other. Your mom signed for the letter I sent you at the post office. I hope you get it. I heard some song lyrics today while I was listening to this Christian radio station in the car:

When you see broken beyond repair, I see healing beyond belief. When you see too far gone, I see one step away from home. When you see nothing but damaged goods, I see something good in the making. We're not finished yet. When you see wounded, I see mended.

Prov. 18:21 "Death and life are in the power of the tongue, and those who love it will eat its fruits." My prayer: Teach us to use our words to give life. Help us to keep quiet when we need to and to speak in love and gentleness when necessary.

Hugs and kisses, Tan.

Twelve

Let It Be

Tanyah didn't seem to have a care in the world that weekend. She got to spend some quality time with the twins and they even went roller-skating together for the first time in almost a whole year. She'd texted one of her coworkers to come as well and he brought his family too. Tanyah tried to do the speed-skating race like she used to do when she was younger, but quickly realized that it was no longer something she should be attempting. They stuck with red light, green light and could barely walk when they all left. Everyone had been sliding all over the floor while trying to start and stop skating in order to win.

She talked to her little sister, Renee, on the phone for a few hours that Sunday just to catch up since they hadn't really talked in a couple of weeks except for short text messages. They spent the majority of the conversation laughing and clowning around as usual. Before they got off the phone, Renee

That One Time My Mother-in-Law Kidnapped My Husband

told her that she'd actually spoken to Taurrean's sister.

"What?" Tanyah asked.

"Yeah, she actually picked up."

"What did she say? How is Taurrean doing? Why isn't anyone talking to me?"

"Girl, she was just mad and acting stupid. She said to tell you that Taurrean is fine and to stop calling and sending the police to their house because they just want to be left alone."

"Fuck that. We'll see how alone they want to be left when I pop up on their asses next week as soon as school is out."

"You're going up there? The parents didn't say anything about it."

"I plan to drive up there over my Christmas break, I just hadn't asked mom and dad to keep the twins yet since I didn't know what their dad and his family had planned. You know they're last minute and shit."

"You're right. Well, don't go up there acting crazy."

"Me?" Tanyah asked innocently.

"Yes, bitch. You. With your crazy ass," Renee said as they both busted out laughing.

On Monday morning, Tanyah received a call at work from Taurrean's former divorce attorney, Mrs. Ramsey. His ex-wife had filed for child support before he'd gone into the hospital, but they had been able to delay the court proceedings all year. Tanyah had stopped sending her money after he left the hospital and went to Georgia, but that wasn't her problem to deal with anymore.

Mrs. Ramsey said that she had been trying to reach him but couldn't. Tanyah gave her the number to one of the hospitals that she suspected Taurrean had been and told her to call back if she needed anything else. She'd used the process of

Let It Be

elimination by calling almost all of them and had a hunch about where he was since the staff refused to give her information and never had anyone call her back.

She called Tanyah back about an hour later saying that the staff told her that he was not listed as being checked in to that hospital and couldn't give her any other information. Tanyah briefly explained to her what had been going on and told her to try calling his parents instead. She gave Mrs. Ramsey their numbers and told her once again to let her know if she was able to speak to him.

Tanyah motioned to Kinsey to watch the class as she stepped into the hallway to answer as her phone rang.

"Hey, Tanyah. What is going on?" Mrs. Ramsey asked plainly.

"Other than what I've already told you, nothing. Why? What happened?" Tanyah asked.

"I called his father, Rick. I told him who I was and that I was calling for Taurrean to discuss his case and a few updates that I had," she started.

"Okay. And?"

"He said that he didn't know who Taurrean was and hung up on me."

"Wait. What?" Tanyah asked in shock.

"So, I called his mother, Evelyn, instead. She told me that his child support case had been dropped, but that she would have him call me."

"I don't know why his dad would say something like that. That's weird. He probably thought that you were calling because of me or something."

"Well, what I find strange is that his mother is saying that the case has been dropped but in order to do that the court has to notify both attorneys. Neither of us have heard anything from our clients," Mrs. Ramsey dictated.

"Honestly, I'd just wait for him to call you and just don't work on the case or do anything until he does. His mother has her hands all in his business and you'll never get to talk to him alone anyway until he gets better. Just send a note over to the other attorney and let him know what's going on."

"Okay, Mrs. Watson. Thanks. I'll talk to you at another time then," Mrs. Ramsey said as they both ended the call.

Tanyah picked the twins up after school that day so that they could go to church with her. They were having their annual Christmas festival event and she had volunteered them all to help out. By the time they got home it was almost 11:00 pm and they were all tired. Tanyah vowed to write Taurrean a short letter about it in her journal once she got up in the morning.

Tuesday, 12-13-16

I had a long, tiring day yesterday, but it was okay. I had to do parking lot attendant duty for the church Christmas festival thing. It's a really cool event, actually. They have like twelve live scenes with backgrounds and people from the church that depict the life, death, and resurrection of Jesus in the scenes. People ride on a hay ride around to each scene and they have speakers reading scripture that goes with the scene and narrates it. I was in a scene one year, but I ended up with a bunch of annoying kids and teenagers so I said never again! I hope to see or hear from you soon.

P.S. If every couple quit when marriage got difficult, one hundred percent of couples would be divorced. Challenges in marriage are an opportunity to work together; not an excuse to give up on each other.

Love, Tan.

Let It Be

Tanyah closed the journal and finished getting herself and the twins ready for school. She headed off to work and decided to treat herself to Burger King for some breakfast croissants like she and Taurrean used to do. Since they were still two for four dollars, she decided to save the second one for her planning period and would eat it as a late lunch. Tanyah always went for a little random excitement, so she got one strawberry jelly and one grape jelly so that she could switch it up and not feel like she was eating the same thing twice. Luckily, she had started to get her appetite back, because she really loved eating breakfast food.

While she was on her planning period, she remembered that she needed to call their health insurance. Tanyah hadn't received an explanation of benefits letter that month and hadn't spoken to them since the beginning of November. She usually talked to them at least once a month to keep up with their deductibles and out-of-pocket expenses. Sheryl picked up on the third ring.

"Hey, Sheryl. It's Tanyah Watson. How are you?" Tanyah replied to Sherly's customary greeting.

"Oh, hi, Tanyah. I'm fine, how are you? I'm so sorry again. I did send you a copy of that death certificate like you'd asked the other day," Sheryl said with concern in her voice.

"Huh? I didn't talk to you the other day. I think you're mistaken. It's me, Tanyah Watson. We last spoke in early November," Tanyah said to her and then continued, "Are you saying that you sent me a DEBT certificate? I haven't been getting my mail and I'm just now getting around to calling so that I can make sure the medical premiums got paid," she rambled before getting cut off.

"No, you requested a copy of his death certificate. I'm sorry,

That One Time My Mother-in-Law Kidnapped My Husband

Tanyah. Let me double check my files real quick," Sheryl said as she began typing furiously on her keyboard, "Yes, Tanyah Watson. Your husband is Taurrean Watson. You called and spoke to me on Monday."

Tanyah was frustrated as hell as she answered, "Sheryl, I don't know what you're talking about, but I assure you that you have not spoken to me since November. Wait, are you saying that my husband is dead?!" Tanyah was now yelling.

"Um. No, I think I'm looking at the wrong account."

"What is going on? What are you saying that you sent me? Because I didn't get anything. And what the hell is a debt certificate anyway? Are we going into collections? Or are you saying "DEATH certificate?"

"Tanyah, let me put you on a brief hold," Sheryl responded without waiting for her to agree.

Tanyah waited on hold for what seemed like forever, and it really was a long time. Sheryl kept her waiting for about fifteen minutes before the connection was restored.

"Hello, Mrs. Watson? This is Tabitha. I'm one of the supervisors here. Sheryl said you had a few questions for me?" a new woman spoke through the phone.

"I had questions, yes; but, I didn't request to speak to a supervisor. I'm just trying to figure out what the hell is going on. Sheryl thinks that she spoke to me the other day and she didn't. She's saying that I either requested a death certificate or a debt certificate and I have no fucking clue what she's talking about either way because, again, I have not talked to her in a month! I just called today after realizing that I haven't been getting my mail and I needed to know if our premiums were still being paid."

"So, I'm sorry, Mrs. Watson, but, at this point, you're going

Let It Be

to have to call your husband's employer. You need to speak to them," Tabitha said.

"For what? Don't you all handle the insurance? Is it paid or not?" Tanyah asked, now exasperated.

"Ma'am, we can't speak to you regarding this situation anymore."

"What situation? You haven't even said anything!" Tanyah yelled into the phone.

"Mrs. Watson, please call his job."

"Fine. But do I owe money or not?" Tanyah asked one last time.

"No, ma'am. The premiums are all paid up and you all have met your deductible. You will not receive any more bills. I will make sure that we resend the explanation of benefits letter to your address on file."

"Thanks," Tanyah said as she hung up the phone.

Tanyah found the number for the human resources department at Taurrean's job by going online and logging into his work account. He hadn't changed any of his passwords or information, plus she was the one who initially set it up when he transferred. Ginger answered the phone and Tanyah explained her disturbing encounter with the insurance company. She asked Ginger if she knew what was going on and why they'd instructed Tanyah to call.

Ginger seemed shocked and said that she hadn't spoken to anyone. She wasn't sure why they told Tanyah to call, but promised to find out and call her back as soon as she knew something. She took down Tanyah's contact information before apologizing for the confusion and then hanging up.

Tanyah sat for a few minutes and then had an idea. Yolanda always knew something about everything going on with

That One Time My Mother-in-Law Kidnapped My Husband

Taurrean and his insurance at any given time. She hadn't talked to her since right after Taurrean had left. She found Yolanda's number in her phone and called. She greeted her warmly as always and asked how she could help. Tanyah explained what was going on and Yolanda was just as confused as Tanyah. She searched her end of the system and said that she didn't see anything out of the ordinary but that she would keep looking and call Tanyah back if she found or heard anything.

When she got home, Tanyah called her parents and talked to them about what was going on. They tried contacting Taurrean's family again, but they never answered for anyone. Tanyah let them know that Renee had just talked to his sister that Sunday, but something felt off. She let them know that she was sure Yolanda would call her back because of the relationship that they had, and she would fill them in on whatever news she relayed. Tanyah suspected they were moving him around to different hospitals trying to throw her off track so that she couldn't find him. She knew what she had to do next.

Tanyah woke up early the next morning. It was Wednesday, the day before game day, and she'd forgotten to grab cash from the bank. The basketball team usually got boxed lunches for the kids to eat before the games so that they wouldn't be hungry after school while they were waiting to play. They had to turn in the money the day before, so that the order could be placed ahead of time. Tanyah ran down the street to the gas station and bought some gummies for each of the twins and got some cash back. She packed it all in their regular lunch box and wrote them some quick I love you notes.

She got ready for work and headed to her car. She felt compelled to pray over herself that day, so she sat in the car

Let It Be

for a few minutes before taking off. Tanyah waited for about an hour to receive a phone call from any of the people who'd said that they would call her back. She thought about calling them, but decided that she needed to take matters into her own hands and escalate the issue. Either Taurrean, his parents, or his sister were going to call Tanyah today, one way or another. She was going to force them to speak to her.

Tanyah got her students started on their assignment and then looked up the phone number for the Clayton County police department. She walked over to Kinsey's desk.

"Hey, girl," Tanyah spoke softly to her.

"Hey, what do you need?" Kinsey replied quietly since she knew that there could possibly be more drama.

"I'm gonna step out into the hallway to call the local police in Georgia. Give me a few minutes, but I'll be right outside."

"Yes, of course. Take your time," she whispered quickly.

Tanyah dialed the phone number that she'd found and waited for someone to pick up.

"Clayton County Police Department, Officer Duncan speaking. How can I direct your call?"

"Good morning, Officer Duncan. My name is Tanyah Watson and I live in Fort Worth, Texas. But, I need to file a missing person's report for my husband, Taurrean Watson, who is currently there in Georgia."

"Okay, um. Give me a second, I can help you. Okay, can you give me a little background information?" the officer asked calmly.

Tanyah briefly walked through what had been going on, just giving him the highlights so that he had an idea of why she was filing the missing person's report. She was giving him Taurrean's family's address when her call waiting beeped in.

That One Time My Mother-in-Law Kidnapped My Husband

She asked the officer to hold on while she removed the phone from her ear to see who was calling. It was one of the Blue Cross Blue Shield phone numbers.

"Officer Duncan, this is someone from our insurance calling. I need to take this, can I put you hold for just a moment? They might have more information that I can give you," Tanyah rushed.

"Yes, ma'am. I'll be right here."

"Hello?" Tanyah answered the call expectantly.

"Hey, Tanyah. It's Yolanda."

"Oh, hey! Did you find anything out? What is going on?"

There was a brief silence and Tanyah thought that maybe the call had dropped so she called out to her, "Yolanda? You still there?"

"I'm so sorry, Tanyah," Yolanda started and her voice cracked, "I don't know what's really going on. I was instructed not to call or talk to you, but you know we've become really close, so I had to."

"Yolanda, what the hell is going on?"

"I don't know why no one will call you back or speak to you. I'm probably gonna lose my job if they find out, but I just... I'm so sorry. Tanyah, your husband died last week on Friday," Yolanda choked out, now crying through the phone.

"What?" Tanyah barely got the words out as a whisper.

"I'm sorry. I'm so, so sorry," Yolanda repeated.

"Oh... Um... Okay," Tanyah stuttered as she felt something in her brain snap out of place.

Yolanda hung up the call on her end and Officer Duncan asked if Tanyah was there. The phone fell from her hands onto the floor as she let out a guttural, agonizing scream that could be heard throughout her hallway and the next one over.

Let It Be

Kinsey came running out of the classroom and caught Tanyah as she fell crying loudly to the floor.

"What is it? What happened? Tanyah?!" Kinsey yelled as she held onto her.

"Dead," Tanyah said through her sobs, "He's dead."

"Hello? Can anyone hear me?" the phone had switched to speaker and Kinsey picked it up to answer.

"Hello?"

"Yes, this is Officer Duncan. I was speaking to Mrs. Tanyah Watson."

"Yes, sir. This is Kinsey, I'm her co-teacher here at school. I think she just found out that her husband died. Can I get your information and call you back? Just hold on for a second. Don't hang up."

Multiple teachers were now standing outside of their doors with a few students looking to see what was going on. Tanyah was still on the floor wailing as the math teacher next door, Mr. Gregg, walked over.

"Come on, Tanyah. Let me help you up," he said softly, as he bent his thin, six foot frame over her.

Tanyah looked up at him from the ground and closed her eyes, still crying as he effortlessly lifted her up and carried her down the hall to the counselor's office. Mr. Gregg got her into a chair and propped her up against the conference table. Her cries were becoming a soft whimper and she was on the verge of passing out. Tanyah laid her head down on the table and stared at the wall on the far side of the room. The counselors were all scrambling in the office when they got there and one quickly grabbed a bottle of water to keep her alert.

Everyone was talking at the same time, but all Tanyah heard were muffled voices. In her mind, she was in the ocean,

That One Time My Mother-in-Law Kidnapped My Husband

treading water right beneath the surface, unable to come up for air. She gazed up at the imaginary waves as they crashed over her head. The foamy white bubbles, paired with the mix of clear and blue water reflecting from the sky overwhelmed her. Her lips parted as she imagined allowing the water to fill her lungs and drown her.

"Mrs. Watson? Tanyah!" Mrs. Thomas, one of the counselors, yelled her name, "We need you to sit up and breathe."

Tanyah snapped out of her hallucination, wiped her face, and stood up. She cleared her throat as she spoke, "I apologize for the fuss. Please get my purse and keys from the classroom," she stated plainly to Kinsey, who quickly left the room.

"Tanyah? Are you okay? Please, sit down for us," Mrs. Blake, one of the other counselors, begged, as she pushed the water bottle closer to her side of the table.

"I'm fine. Please tell the office that I need to leave," Tanyah said as Kinsey walked back into the office.

"Where are you going? You shouldn't be alone," Kinsey asked her.

Tanyah looked at everyone, confused, and tilted her head to the side as she spoke calmly, "Where do you think I'm going?" Tanyah half-smiled tightly, "They killed my husband. I'm going to Georgia; and, I'm going to kill them all."

She grabbed her phone from Kinsey and reached for her purse. Mrs. Thomas reached for it as well and got it before Tanyah could.

"Mrs. Watson. Please," Mrs. Thomas quietly urged her.

"Mrs. Thomas. My purse," Tanyah said, defiantly.

"Tanyah. You're in shock. Sit down. Now," the counselor said to her sternly as Kinsey helped her back to the table.

Let It Be

Mrs. Blake called the main office, and got Tanyah's emergency contact information from her file. She called Tanyah's parents from her desk phone and let them know what happened. She handed Tanyah the phone as she sat back down and broke all over again. Her stoic demeanor crumbled and tears ran freely down her face, but she didn't make a sound.

"Hello?" Tanyah said into the receiver.

"Hey, Tanyah. Your counselor told us what happened. I'm so sorry. But we need you to stay put and don't go driving across the country," her mom said through the phone.

"Okay, mom," Tanyah replied back, starting to sob.

Her dad sighed heavily, "It's okay, baby girl. It's going to be okay."

"They killed him, dad," Tanyah cried into the phone.

"We're coming. Promise me that you're not going to leave work and drive to Georgia."

"I promise, dad. I won't go."

"Okay, just stay there. We're on our way. We love you," her mom said.

To keep Tanyah occupied, and to hopefully help her get to the bottom of everything, the counselors had called in the campus police officer. He had Tanyah tell him the whole story of what had been going on for the past few months. She was able to step outside of her body and tell him what happened as everyone else listened to details that they had not been privy to before. They all sat silently in disbelief as she spoke. It was as though she were describing someone else's account of the events; her voice was distant and her gaze was far off.

Her parents must have been speeding down the highway, because they arrived in a little less than two hours on a two and a half hour drive. Her mom hugged her tight when she

That One Time My Mother-in-Law Kidnapped My Husband

saw her as her dad thanked everyone in the office for calling them. Kinsey found the obituary online and printed it out along with the information for the funeral home.

Tanyah's parents asked her if she was okay to drive, and she assured them that she was. They followed her back to her apartment to discuss what their next steps should be. For a while, she just stood in the middle of her living room crying and letting her dad hold her.

Once she was calm, Tanyah informed them that Taurrean's job was about thirty minutes away in Grapevine, and she knew one of the other supervisors that he worked with. She needed to speak to him and find out what was going on since the human resources department had never called her back.

Tanyah found the main office and asked for Matt. She hadn't met him in person yet, but she knew all about him from conversations with Taurrean and she knew that he and one of the other supervisors had visited him in the hospital. He let Tanyah know that he hadn't spoken to anyone other than the HR department and that all they told him was that Taurrean had died. He said that he found it odd that Tanyah hadn't reached out, but understood. She told him briefly a little bit about what was going on and he stared at her blinking, not believing the story that he was listening to.

Matt informed them of where the human resources office was located and it turned out to be less than ten miles from Tanyah's apartment. She told them all that she needed to go to the actual office and talk to them in person. She gave Matt her number, as well as her parents' information and let him know that one of them would keep him updated. He gave her a quick hug.

They all hopped back into her parents' car and quickly

Let It Be

headed back towards Tanyah's side of town so that they could get there before everyone left for the day. They were brought into the empty cafeteria and waited at a table. A tall woman came out and introduced herself as Ginger and shook everyone's hand. Tanyah skipped the pleasantries and got straight to the point.

"Why did you lie to me?"

"I'm so sorry, Mrs. Watson," she started.

"I don't care how sorry you are. You knew my husband was dead and didn't say anything. What is going on and who have you spoken to?"

"I apologize, Mrs. Watson. You caught us off guard when you called. Someone else has been impersonating you and requesting information. I have also confirmed this with Tabitha from the insurance company, whom you've already spoken to as well. Whoever it was that called, they had all of the correct identification. We've never had something like this happen before and I had to contact my bosses, as I'm sure you understand. While we can't share with you what all has been sent, we can now confirm that it was not sent to your home address and we now know that it was not you who requested any of it. We will have to deal with it internally from this point. I really am sorry that I could not contact you sooner. Taurrean was a great man and we were all very sad to hear of his passing. A few of us went to see him while he was in the hospital and we were really hoping that he would get better."

"From now on, if someone calls saying that they are me, you need to confirm that it actually is me. I don't care if we have to set up a secret password, a damn handshake, or what, but you better not allow this to happen again," Tanyah stated plainly.

"We understand. Again, we're so sorry," Ginger repeated.

That One Time My Mother-in-Law Kidnapped My Husband

They talked a while longer and Ginger gave her a folder with all of Taurrean's benefits and life insurance information. She told her who she needed to call and let her know that they would be expecting the call and to let them know that she'd spoken to Ginger. She said they would guide her through the rest of the process and tell her what other documents they needed.

After they left, her dad took them out to eat. Tanyah ended up taking most of it back home as left-overs. Her appetite was non-existent. She couldn't figure out how she was going to be able to tell the twins. She didn't know how she was going to tell anyone. She still didn't even know what happened. Everyone would ask and she wouldn't have any answers. They would be more concerned with the details, than the fact that he was dead. She was a widow at thirty-four years old.

Her parents called Porsha to come over while they all waited for the kids to get home from school. Tanyah sat on the couch in silence while Porsha and her parents talked. She was having an out of body experience. This couldn't be happening to her. He couldn't be dead.

Porsha sat with her until it was time for the kids to start getting home from riding the bus. Tanyah's dad let Porsha know that he and her mom would be leaving later that evening because he had an appointment in the morning, but they would be back for the twins basketball game. He asked her if Tanyah and twins could all stay the night with her so that they wouldn't be alone and of course she happily agreed. Tanyah told her that she would text her when they were on the way.

Porsha headed back to her apartment as the twins were racing up to the door. They'd seen their grandparents' car and were already screaming their names in excitement. They

Let It Be

came in talking a mile a minute as usual and telling their grandparents about their day at school. Once they were done talking and eating, Tanyah called them over to the couch to sit with her. Tears ran down her face as she told the twins that Taurrean had died.

The girls hugged her and cried. Then they started wiping the tears from Tanyah's face and asking if she was okay. She cried a little harder as she told them that she wasn't. Her parents hugged the girls and told them that everything was going to be alright. Tanyah didn't know what to say when they asked about the funeral as she realized she had no clue when it was or if it had even happened already. She didn't want to lie to them.

Once they were all semi-calmed down, Tanyah told them to shower and pack an overnight bag because they were all having a sleepover at Porsha's house. The twins' eyes got big and they smiled hard. Her parents let the girls know that they had to leave, but would be back the next day for the basketball game. That news cheered them up even more and they ran to go get ready after giving them one last hug and kiss. Tanyah walked her parents to their car and told them to drive safely. She promised to head straight to Porsha's house as soon as the twins were ready.

When they were finished they all headed over to Porsha's house. Her husband, Josh, was home and he gave Tanyah a huge hug as she walked in. Porsha sent the girls to Brandie's room and told them to start setting up all of the blankets. Once they ran back, she told Tanyah that she'd just told her kids what happened and they were in the other room and had been crying so they just needed a minute. Tanyah made herself comfortable on the couch and started flipping through the TV

That One Time My Mother-in-Law Kidnapped My Husband

channels.

They let the kids play for a while before bed and they all came out to give them hugs. It was nice getting double hugs. Tanyah held back her tears until they had all ran back to their rooms. Porsha sat with her for a couple of hours before she had to turn in for the night as well. She offered to take off from work, but Tanyah told her that she would be okay.

Tanyah scrolled through Facebook for a while, debating what she should say. She typed and then deleted unfinished posts multiple times. She couldn't bring herself to post anything about Taurrean dying. She quietly cried herself to sleep that night, not knowing how she was going to make it.

The next morning, her parents called to check on her and let her know that they would be on their way back into town later that afternoon. Tanyah let them know that she would be hanging out at Porsha's house for a while and then she was going to head back to her apartment once the kids all left for school. She also had a few phone calls that she needed to make before getting her day started and she was hell bent on finding something to keep herself busy.

Tanyah called her best friend, Nicole, to tell her what happened. They talked for a long time and Nicole let Tanyah know that she was going to grab one of her kids out of school, talk to her husband, and then she'd be on her way later that afternoon. Tanyah thanked her for always being there for her and of course cried again for the thousandth time before getting off the phone. She still needed to do something to occupy her time. Tanyah put on some workout clothes and went for a run.

She ran and prayed and listened to gospel music for about three miles before feeling like she could think clearly. She stopped over a small bridge that was deep in the woods and slightly off of the regular trail. She'd found it by accident early one morning while she was running away from some crazy squirrels and came from time to time just to stare at the water and regroup. She'd only shown Taurrean and the twins her "secret spot." It was too special to just share with anyone.

Tanyah stood in the center of the bridge and tilted her head back, allowing the sun to kiss her face as she closed her eyes. She let the tears fall down her face and prayed for the pain to subside. She watched a family of ducks paddle across the small body of water and then decided to head back to her apartment. She stopped by her garage and decided to grab the Christmas tree while she was there. With everything that had been going on, she'd completely forgotten about it and wanted to make sure that the twins still got to have some fun decorating.

Tanyah tuckered herself out just enough to be able to take a shower and a nap before anyone was set to arrive. Her sleep was restless and she had dreams of Taurrean calling out and trying to find her, but never being able to reach her. She woke up disturbed and afraid to be alone. She felt haunted. Luckily, her parents were now on their way back to her apartment and she had the twins' basketball game to look forward to. Nicole would be meeting them there and she couldn't wait to see her best friend.

Tanyah decided to go ahead and post the news of Taurrean's passing on Facebook. She needed to get it out of the way, plus their friends and the people who helped them the most during all of the cancer treatments deserved to know. There was no way she could bring herself to call everyone individually.

She stopped and started multiple times. Tanyah prayed and cried as she typed the words that she thought would convey

That One Time My Mother-in-Law Kidnapped My Husband

the love she had for him and not the hate that she felt.

There are no words to describe the brokenness and heartbreak I feel at this time after losing the love of my life, my best friend, my amazing husband, Taurrean.

I've been his biggest fan since we were ten years old and even more so these last few months together. We fought his cancer side by side alongside friends and family that loved us both so much. No one was more brave, trusting, and as strong as my sweetheart, my hero.

He's now with our Father in Heaven, who loves him even more than I do; and, as a believer, even I can't imagine loving him more than I already do. The love God has for us is unfathomable and I rejoice and praise God for allowing me to have Taurrean and share in His love for him if even for just a short while.

I miss you so much, Babes, and I wish you were still here; but, I know the confident hope we have in Christ and that you'll be waiting on me when I get there. I've loved you my whole life, always will, and forever.

Tanyah's parents arrived not too long after and they all sat in her living room talking and watching TV. She snuggled up to her dad on the couch where she felt safe and he put his arm around her. The show Criminal Minds was on since that was pretty much the only show that she and the twins watched on that TV and they had a good time speculating and distracting themselves from everything that happened for a little while before it was time to leave.

Nicole called as they were on their way to the twins' school and let Tanyah know that she was in town and wouldn't be far behind them when they arrived. Tanyah and her parents waited in the parking lot for her when they arrived. She was only about five minutes away and Tanyah laughed to herself thinking about how Nicole was probably driving crazy like she used to in high school. Any time she rode in the car with Nicole to Walmart, Nicole always hit all of the curbs on the twisted road.

Tanyah ran to her car when she saw her pull up and almost dragged her out of the driver's seat when she opened the door to give her a hug. She'd brought her daughter with her, and she was in the back smiling the cutest smile in the world and watching the emotional exchange.

They all walked into the gym and Tanyah was surprised to see that Tommy and most of his family were also at the game. His mom hadn't been to one of the twins' games in a long time. Tommy hadn't frequented too many himself, but his dad showed up more often than not. Two of his sisters were there and they all seemed in good spirits as they waved to Tanyah and her family.

This game was the last one that the team had before the Christmas break and it was sure to be a good one. Tanyah was glad that they'd all showed up and that the girls and their team would have a really loud cheering section. Of course Nicole and Tanyah were quietly talking shit and laughing the whole time.

The team played hard and the girls each had multiple points. As always, Kayla was in the double digits and showcased some amazing ball handling skills. She tended to show out and show off whenever their dad was at a game. Kaylyn had several steals and some wide open three-pointers that had the crowd going wild as well. The whole team held their own, and started pulling away in the last quarter. They won by about fifteen points and the stands went crazy as one of their teammates, Gianna, a skinny white girl who played like she was already

That One Time My Mother-in-Law Kidnapped My Husband

in the WNBA, hit a three-point shot at the buzzer from about four feet beyond the three-point line. Gianna was a beast and Tanyah could hardly wait to see them all play in high school.

Tanyah's dad had been talking to Tommy and his family throughout the game. That was just the kind of man he was. He never held a grudge, even when he should, and he was friendly to everyone he encountered. They all stood around afterwards talking and her former mother-in-law came up to her to give her a hug. She told her that she was sorry to hear that Tanyah's husband had passed away.

Tanyah was almost numb to it all and didn't cry. Instead she gave them all a small smile and a genuine thank you. Tommy gave her a hug and she froze with her hands at her side, not really knowing what to do.

"Let me know if you need anything," Tommy said as he looked into her eyes.

He seemed serious. All Tanyah could do was nod her head. She glanced over at Nicole and saw her discreetly mouth the words, "Bitch, what?" and quickly looked down so that she wouldn't start laughing. The exchange was out of character, but maybe it was a sign of them possibly being cordial and able to move past all of the hate and craziness in the future. She didn't plan to hold her breath on it though.

As the twins came out, the whole family cheered like they had just won a national championship game and Tanyah smiled. The girls were cheesing, laughing, and soaking up all of the attention. She loved how much support they had and was glad that everyone was getting along and there wasn't any drama. Tanyah wouldn't have been able to handle any more stress.

Her parents decided to drive back home that evening since Nicole was staying with her for the night. Tanyah and the

Let It Be

twins rode home with Nicole and her parents left from the school in their car. The girls had a half-day at school the next day and then they would be starting their Christmas break. Tanyah hadn't been back to work yet and she was glad to have two weeks off to regroup.

A few people had tried to reach out and call her, but she ignored most calls or sent a text message back instead. One of her former co-workers had heard the news and called her out of the blue. They hadn't talked in almost a year. It had been a rude exchange on Tanyah's end, but in her defense, she thought that people should know better. She told Nicole about the conversation on their way home from the game when she asked if anyone had reached out to her.

"Girl, one of my old co-workers called. We haven't even talked in a whole minute and she's all like "Oh my God, girl what happened?" And I said "Bitch, my husband died, what the fuck do you think happened?" and I hung up on her ass," Tanyah recalled.

"Oh. Well," Nicole let her words trail off as she laughed and shook her head.

Once they arrived back at the apartment, Tanyah had the girls shower and let them stay up for a little while with Nicole's little girl and start decorating the Christmas tree while they sat and talked. Nicole said that some of their high school friends were wanting to start a Go Fund Me campaign to help Tanyah out with any expenses she might need. She was never one to ask for help and couldn't bring herself to accept. She had no clue if she would even need financial assistance, and didn't want to ask not knowing for sure. Nicole thanked them all and told everyone to hold off until Tanyah gave them the green light.

That One Time My Mother-in-Law Kidnapped My Husband

* * *

The next morning, Tanyah called Vanessa, who was not only one of her co-workers, but also like her spiritual work mother. She had walked through all of this with Tanyah since the very beginning and always prayed with her and for her. Vanessa treated her like one of her own children, who were around the same age.

The funeral home had finally posted the burial date and it was scheduled for Saturday. Vanessa asked if Tanyah was going and she told her that she hadn't even been notified. Vanessa gave her a bunch of information about how the funeral process was supposed to work and Tanyah had no clue that it was against the law for Taurrean's family to bury him without her consent since they were still married.

Tanyah thanked her for the information and called her parents on speaker phone so that Nicole could listen in and join the conversation. She told them about finding out that the funeral was the next day and how they couldn't legally do it without her. Tanyah didn't even want to go at this point, but the principle of it all was bothering her. She didn't want to be vindictive, but she had to find out what was going on.

She deserved to know and she deserved a say in what was happening. At the very least she deserved to be invited to her own husband's funeral since no one had even bothered to call and tell her that he'd died almost a whole week ago. Sharee had even lied to Renee saying that Taurrean didn't want to talk to Tanyah just the other day and he was already dead. His mom did the same thing when she'd told his lawyer that he would call her back.

Tanyah let them all know that she was going to send a fax and

Let It Be

request that the funeral home director call her back as soon as they received it so that she could find out what happened. Tanyah had to wait until 9 am for the main office of her apartment complex to open and then walked over to speak to the manager. She let her know what happened and asked to be able to use their fax machine. They were happy to allow it and made sure she knew that they would help in any way she needed.

Tanyah put together some documents that included a copy of her marriage certificate, driver's license, social security card, her apartment lease contract, and a certificate from their premarital counseling course for good measure. On the cover letter she addressed the funeral director and let them know who she was. She requested that they send her any and all documents related to Taurrean's burial service and informed them that she had not given nor had she been asked to give consent for these services. Tanyah listed all of her contact information including her address, phone number, and email and then sent the fax.

She waited for a delivery confirmation before walking back to her apartment to wait for the phone call. She ate a little bit and added a few more decorations to the Christmas tree while her and Nicole waited anxiously for the funeral home to call. Tanyah gave it an hour before she told Nicole to go ahead and call her parents back and relay messages back and forth while Tanyah called the funeral home.

The secretary answered after a few rings, "Hello, Cokely Funeral Home. How can I help you?"

"Good morning. My name is Tanyah Watson, and I'm calling about an urgent matter that needs to be addressed with the director. I'd like to speak with him or her please."

That One Time My Mother-in-Law Kidnapped My Husband

"His name is Anthony Cokely, I'll transfer you to his office now," the woman said politely as she put Tanyah on hold.

"Hello, this is Anthony Cokely," an older man said as he picked up the line.

"Hi, Mr. Cokely, this is Tanyah Watson."

"Yes, I spoke to you last week. How can I help you?"

"Mr. Cokely, you did not speak to me last week," Tanyah said as she looked over at Nicole, whose eyes got big as she relayed what was happening to Tanyah's parents.

"No, I spoke to you last week and you told me to let your father-in-law handle all of the funeral arrangements and that he would be paying for it. Are you okay?"

"Mr. Cokely," Tanyah started before taking a deep breath. Nicole was scribbling notes that her parents were saying and her dad had said to be calm. They could hear her voice getting louder and more agitated as she continued, "Mr. Cokely, I assure you that you did not speak to me last week because I literally just found out two days ago that my husband died."

There was silence on the other end of the phone so Tanyah spoke again.

"Sir, can you please tell me about the conversation that you believe you had with me?"

"Well, I spoke to your deceased husband's dad and the family said that you were separated and in the middle of a divorce," he began and Nicole grabbed Tanyah's arm to stop her from blowing up so that he could finish talking as she scribbled notes and relayed more messages to Tanyah's parents.

The director quickly cleared his throat and kept talking, "I told him that he needed to have you call me and he said that he would. I was out of the office, but got a message to call you."

Tanyah interrupted his story and asked, "What phone num-

Let It Be

ber were you told to contact me on?"

Some papers ruffled before he spoke again, "It was area code 254-334-2403."

"Mr. Cokely, the phone number that you were told to call is my now deceased husband's cell phone number. I have listed all of my information on the fax that I sent to your office this morning. Have you checked it?"

"Give me a second, we don't normally get faxes, so I haven't looked," he said hurriedly.

Tanyah put her phone on mute so that he couldn't hear her talking back and forth with Nicole and her parents. Everyone was dumbfounded and could hardly believe the lengths that Taurrean's family was going to not only hide the fact that he had died from her, but also impersonating her in his absence. She couldn't figure out a motive or purpose.

Mr. Cokely got back on the line and his attitude changed. He sounded irritated as he spoke callously, "Okay, Mrs. Watson, I understand that it was not you and I now have your information. What do you want me to do with the body?"

"I'm not giving my consent to bury him. I am going to be traveling to your office, but I'm coming from Texas so it will take me a day. I would like to meet with you to discuss cremation or whatever other options that I have. But again, I'm not giving anyone permission to bury my husband without me there."

"Okay, Mrs. Watson. I'll call you back in about five or ten minutes," he said, hanging up the phone before allowing Tanyah to say anything else.

Tanyah got up and began pacing the room. She was hot and almost hyperventilating. How the hell could this be happening? And for what? She heard Nicole and her parents

That One Time My Mother-in-Law Kidnapped My Husband

talking in the background and she plopped down on the couch to catch her breath. She was telling her parents about their friends offering to help financially and how she thought it could be beneficial, especially now. They ended the phone call a few minutes later and she told them that she'd call back when they heard something.

Nicole sat down next to Tanyah and told her that another one of their friends had offered to help. Tanyah relented and said that it was okay with her if they did the campaign. She didn't know what the funeral expenses would cost and they didn't have burial insurance. She also didn't know what was going on with his job and the life insurance she'd made him get after everything that had happened with the HR department. Plus, she would need to pay for travel expenses going halfway across the country.

She wanted to fly, but didn't have the money right then, and she needed her parents to go with her. Tanyah's dad suggested that they drive his RV instead to save on money for flight tickets and a hotel. He was considered a disabled vet in the military so he got to park for free in most RV parks. Tanyah had driven it before so she could help him drive.

An hour of planning had passed and she still hadn't received the call back so she called the funeral home once again. Tanyah reconfirmed with the director that she was not consenting to the burial and he affirmed everything that she said. He told her that he had another funeral to attend to, but that he would call her back in about three hours. She asked if he'd still be in the office since it would be after hours and he said that he would, so she told him that she'd be awaiting his call later and let him go.

The twins would already be with Tommy and his family for

Let It Be

the first part of the Christmas break so she didn't have to make any extra arrangements. She called and let him know her plans as a courtesy and he was very amicable and offered to keep them longer if needed. She told him that she planned to be back in time, but she would let him know for sure once she returned. She had an entire week to take care of whatever she needed and she didn't want to stay in Georgia any longer than she absolutely had to.

Tanyah and Nicole went to eat and then hung out for the rest of the day before taking the twins to meet up with their dad once they had gotten everything that they wanted to take with them packed. Tanyah's parents planned to sleep, gas up the RV, and arrive early the next morning so that they could hit the road. Nicole had to get back home to Houston, but wanted to wait for Tanyah to get the returned call from the funeral home.

Tanyah got a call and picked up without looking at the phone screen.

"Hello?"

"Tanyah," Evelyn said her name when she picked up. She sounded like she'd been crying.

"What the hell are you calling for? Are you finally calling to tell me that my husband is dead?!" Tanyah yelled through the phone.

"Please, don't do this. I just want to bury my son. The funeral home said you want to burn him up," she pleaded with Tanyah.

"You're literally having a funeral without me! Don't call my phone, I'll burn your whole family up!" Tanyah yelled again as she hung up in Evelyn's face.

She tried to call back, and Tanyah blocked her number from being able to call.

That One Time My Mother-in-Law Kidnapped My Husband

Sharee tried to call next. Tanyah picked up the phone, called her a fat bitch before she could say anything, and then hung up and blocked her number from calling as well. Tanyah sat with her head in her hands crying for a few minutes before calming herself down and calling her parents. They told her that Evelyn had tried to call them crying as well and begging them to talk to Tanyah. They had basically told her that she needed to talk to Tanyah herself and make things right with her because what they were doing was foul. Tanyah's mom was pissed, and she was sure that she had probably wanted to curse Evelyn out, but she would never tell Tanyah that one way or another.

When Mr. Cokely didn't call, Tanyah called the funeral director back around 10 pm and asked him what was going on.

His attitude was worse than before and he was rude as he spoke, "Look, Mrs. Watson, your husband's family says that they have a will. I will look it over myself in the morning and decide what to do then."

"What do you mean you'll decide what to do? I already told you what you can LEGALLY do, and that is absolutely nothing until I get there. Besides, my husband never executed a will. And, in addition to that, at this point, anything that they say or any documents that they give you should automatically be suspect because you now know that they lied and pretended to be me!" Tanyah yelled through the phone.

"You need to get an attorney and sue the family. Me and my business have nothing to do with your family and your problems. I'll no longer be speaking to you," he said and then hung up in Tanyah's face.

Tanyah looked at the phone in disbelief and tried to call back

Let It Be

but only got the answering machine. She hung up instead of leaving a message and called the police department to file a police report. After informing the officers of what was going on, they took her report down and let her know that they would go up to the funeral home in the morning to investigate. Tanyah let them know that they had to go first thing in the morning because they were planning the funeral for early afternoon and she wouldn't be there yet since she was coming from Texas.

Nicole left the next day as Tanyah and her parents took off in the RV. Tanyah told her dad to start driving first since she didn't want to have to drive over any of the new bridges just yet. She barely felt comfortable in the car going over the spaghetti-like twists and turns in the air.

While she rode, she talked to a few of their family friends who had called to ask her mom how she was doing. Everyone was being strong for her and let her know that they would help her in any way that she needed. Her school even called her mom and let her know that they had also set up a Go Fund Me campaign for any expenses that she might need. Tanyah was overwhelmed with everyone's generosity.

Tanyah spent some time texting back and forth with Steff and Henry and updating them on what was going on. She let them know that she was going out of town to try to handle all of the crazy mess; but, she definitely wanted to go get drinks or something when she got back. She needed their hilarious banter and they had all gotten close.

The police department called to let Tanyah know that they hadn't found any documents with her name on it at the funeral home that day. They told her that they would keep investigating and for her to come straight to their office

That One Time My Mother-in-Law Kidnapped My Husband

building when she arrived. Tanyah tried calling the funeral home again but the secretary would only take a message.

She and her dad switched off driving a couple of times before finally arriving a few hours outside of the city at the RV park that evening. They planned to stay the night there and then drive the rest of the way to the police station in the morning. While her dad was hooking up the RV to all of the water, electric, and sewer lines, Tanyah called her sister, Renee to update her on everything that had happened that day. It was starting to rain and the weather was fitting with her mood.

Tanyah's brother-in-law, Tony, was upset and Renee was so furious she'd been crying and ready to fight. She told Tanyah that she was going to call Sharee and find out what their problem was and probably curse her out as well. Tanyah had been crying throughout the whole conversation but suddenly turned it all off and wiped at her tears and runny nose. She told Renee to make sure she called Sharee a fat bitch before she got off the phone. Tony giggled, but Renee knew Tanyah was dead serious and simply said, "Already" before hanging up the phone. Tanyah's mom shook her head in the background at the whole exchange.

Tanyah had the same restless sleep she'd been having for the past week. She couldn't sleep through the whole night without waking up at the exact same time, 1:10 am, with strange chest pains for a few moments before it subsided and she fell back asleep. She hadn't told anyone about it because she didn't have time to go to the hospital and it was only for a few seconds so it was barely worth mentioning. It was more than likely just stress and she'd deal with it later. Tanyah already knew she was probably going crazy, she didn't need a doctor to tell her that.

Let It Be

Her dad stopped at a McDonald's in the morning to grab them all breakfast and they ate on the road. It was still drizzling when they arrived at the police station. Tanyah told the officer up front who she was and he called out to another officer who she guessed had told them to expect her.

Officer Cato introduced himself to Tanyah and her family and shook her dad's hand. Tanyah caught him up to speed on her end and he informed her that a service had been performed the day before she arrived, but there had not been a burial. Tanyah requested that he escort her and her parents to the funeral home which was less than ten miles away so that she could speak to Mr. Cokely in person. She really hoped that he still had his funky little attitude as well so that maybe her dad would pop him in his smart mouth one good time.

Tanyah walked into the building first and was greeted by the secretary. She didn't bother with pleasantries when Tanyah told her who she was and told her to find Mr. Cokely so that she could speak to him. The officer stood silent but stepped a little closer to Tanyah.

Mr. Cokely entered the room and immediately spoke to all of them, "I have nothing to say to anyone of you."

Tanyah tried her hardest not to fly off the handle, "Mr. Cokely, we spoke on the phone. I'm here to find out what you did with my husband's body and I would like to see him."

"I don't know what you're talking about," he responded to her.

She looked at the officer before continuing, "Mr. Cokely, you have all of my information that I sent to you via fax and here are the actual originals of that same information," she said as she tried to hand him the documents.

The director refused to take any of her documents and stated,

That One Time My Mother-in-Law Kidnapped My Husband

"I plead the fifth."

"You what?" Tanyah raised her voice at his very obvious ignorance and dismissive tone, "Tell me where my husband is, now."

"You need to get a lawyer and I plead the fifth," he said.

"You're not even in court or on trial, you can't plead the fifth! Where is my husband?" Tanyah said more forcefully and balled her fists up at her side.

Officer Cato caught the motion and intervened, "Mr. Cokely, did you speak to Mrs. Watson already and do you have knowledge of where her husband's body is located?"

"I plead the fifth and she needs to contact my lawyers," he responded.

"Well, then what's your lawyer's information then," Tanyah asked, now ready to beat the shit out of him.

"I don't have to tell you that."

"Yes, you do, if you're telling me to contact them. Why won't you just tell me where he is? Please, just let me see him. Is he even here?" Tanyah questioned as she looked at the police officer begging for help.

"I plead the fifth," he repeated as Tanyah started to take a step toward him. She subconsciously stopped with her foot mid-air and was interrupted by Officer Cato's voice.

"Unfortunately, we can't make him give you any information, Mrs. Watson. And we have no proof of any wrongdoing," Officer Cato said to her quietly.

"This is some bullshit," Tanyah said under her breath as she stormed out of the building so that the bastard wouldn't see her break down and cry.

Her parents and the officer followed her outside as she stood in the parking lot with tears running down her face mixed with

Let It Be

heavier rain. She was at a loss of what to do and just wanted to know what was going on. She still hadn't even been told how Taurrean had died or what happened. Her dad talked to the officer briefly and asked him what they should do. He told them to follow him back to the police station so that Tanyah could write a full statement and then he gave them the address and information for some law offices that were open.

Tanyah wrote furiously on the police statement form and had barely scratched the surface of what had been going on that brought her to this point. She asked for another sheet of paper and another officer grabbed it for her. By the time she was finished, Tanyah's written statement was seven pages long. She got up to hand the stack to Officer Cato when she was done.

"What's this?"

"It's my statement," Tanyah said matter-of-factly and looked at him wondering if he'd really forgotten that he'd asked her to write one.

"All of these papers are part of your statement?"

"Yes. It's seven pages, but I assure you that it's all factual information with no added opinions whatsoever."

The other officers all looked at her parents and her dad just shrugged her shoulders.

"Okay, well we will file this statement with your previous reports and I'll personally be the one following up with you," Officer Cato said after he'd read through all of the statement forms.

He wrote down all of the information and directions on how to get to the law offices that he'd told them about and also gave Tanyah, as well as her parents, one of his business cards and included his cell phone number on the back. He didn't wish them luck, but instead said that he would be praying for them and wished them a safe trip back to Texas. He promised to be in touch once he got more information and gave them a copy of her police statement forms to take with them.

About fifteen minutes later, they pulled around to the back of a law office building. There were multiple offices and most had adjoining doors on the inside. Tanyah and her family stepped into the first office and spoke to one of the attorneys. They explained the situation and what was going on. Of course, the attorney called in her counterparts and all of them listened intently at the unbelievable story that they were being told.

The slim, red-headed lady asked them to hold on for a minute while she went next door to another law firm's office. She returned with a couple of the other attorneys and explained the situation. They all wanted to help and were telling Tanyah and her family the next steps to take and what information they would need. The attorneys were all so impacted, that none of them charged a single dime for anything that they were helping her with.

One of the offices sent over a demand letter for information requesting the funeral director's attorney's information as well as confirmation or denial of the burial and burial location. Another office called the county court and had them check for any wills that had been filed for probate and gave them all of Tanyah's information so that she could be contacted as soon as anything came up. One of the secretaries was able to find the information for the hospital where he'd died so that Tanyah could go find out what happened.

At the end of all of the meetings and discussing what was going on, Tanyah was weak. She could barely move and her voice was hardly a whisper. Her parents had to speak for her.

Let It Be

She was numb and didn't know how much more she could take or find out. Her dad decided that they would eat dinner and stay at another RV park for the night and then go to the hospital, recheck the court filings, and meet with the attorneys again the next day after they got some rest. They were all mentally drained.

Tanyah couldn't eat and opted to just lay down and try to sleep instead. She felt herself going down a dark hole that she wasn't sure she'd be able to get out of this time. Every breath she took was filled with anxiety. Hot tears stung her face while her parents consoled her before she finally fell asleep.

The next morning, they went to the courthouse first and spoke with the probate department. A will still hadn't been submitted and Tanyah didn't think that one ever would be. Taurrean didn't have a will and even if his family had tried to execute one after they took him, he wouldn't have been in any acceptable mental or physical state to sign anything given his medications and the health issues that he was having. She double checked all of Tanyah's information and made sure that she had everything she needed to be able to keep in touch in case anything changed.

When they got to the hospital, it was clear that the situation was becoming even more twisted and nefarious than she expected. Tanyah ended up having to speak with the administrators of the hospital just to get any files and records related to Taurrean's death. She'd had enough suspicion to make sure that she brought all of her legal documents with her to prove who she was when they all began to ask questions and basically reveal more lies that had been told. Only this time, instead of pretending to be her, the hospital staff said that Evelyn had told them that Taurrean was not married at all.

Since Tanyah had to once again explain to another company what was going on, and that she had no intentions to stay in Georgia any longer, they allowed her to wait while they gathered all of Taurrean's medical files and paperwork so that she could try to piece together what happened to him. One of the nurses sat with her while she waited, but didn't speak. Tanyah tried to hold it together and was able to keep all but a few tears from escaping. She stared through the TV on the wall until the hospital administrator came back with all of the paperwork they had. Tanyah choked out a weak "Thank you" and her parents shook the man's hand before leaving.

Their next stop was to go back to the lawyer's office to see what information they were able to gather. It turned out that the funeral director didn't have an actual lawyer, he just had basic law coverage through a company that outsourced cases and provided discounts for a monthly fee. Tanyah had the right mind to go back to the funeral home and beat his ass but she was no longer in any shape to fight. The attorneys were able to get a copy of the will that he said the family provided him, and it was evident that there was foul play. His signature wasn't the same and his mother was a notary. The two witness signatures belonged to his sister and her shady boyfriend so nothing about the will seemed legit, especially given the fact that it hadn't been filed in probate court.

Mr. Breeden, the owner of the firm and lead attorney, called Tanyah and her family into his office. He'd gone over all of the information that they provided and wanted to discuss the next steps for them.

"Mrs. Watson, on behalf of my office and the rest of the offices in this building, we just wanted to say how sorry we are for your loss and what you've had to go through," he started and Tanyah nodded for him to continue.

"We all had a meeting and discussed how we thought that this case should be handled. Your in-laws have done quite a bit of illegal damage. In the process, they've roped in some pretty large and unknowing accomplices that span across different states. So far, we have the funeral home, his place of employment, his medical insurance, and I don't know what you found out earlier, but I also suspect the hospital, and if they probate that will, then the courts as well. Mrs. Watson, all of these things are so intricately intertwined that you can't just go after the family on their own."

"What do you mean? The other people didn't know, the only one who did know and refused to do anything about it was the funeral director," Tanyah replied.

"Unfortunately, because of the way that it all occurred, you would have to sue everyone all at the same time. You can't separate them. And, Mrs. Watson, while we've all been more than happy to assist you this far, a case of this magnitude is going to cost you a lot of money," he took a pause and then continued, "Unless we know their end game, be it insurance fraud or something else, you need to decide if it's even worth pursuing."

"We understand," her father said when she didn't respond.

"This is all fresh, and I want you to make an informed decision. So, after you go back to Texas and have some time to really think about it, give me a call and let me know what you want to do. The retainer fee will be $5,000.00 to get started and my firm will be the main one working the case; but, the others agreed to help and provide some of their resources with no additional charges."

That One Time My Mother-in-Law Kidnapped My Husband

"Okay," Tanyah managed to get out before standing up.

"Jessica, is going to be sending you an email with the documents that we were able to get and once we find out where he's been buried we'll get that information out to you as well. She'll also give you the instructions on how to request your own copy of the death certificate in case you're not sure how to do that," Mr. Breeden said as he shook everyone's hand.

They all sat in the RV for a little while trying to decide their next steps. While her parents were talking, Tanyah looked over the paperwork she'd got from the hospital. She scanned through each page trying to make sense of it all. According to the files, Taurrean was brought to the hospital on November 30, 2016 via ambulance and was diagnosed as having distributive shock. She flipped over to the notes from the EMT staff and saw a transcript of the questions they'd asked him along with his answers.

They asked the normal questions about who he was and he was able to answer, but when they began to ask him about where he was, he thought that he was still in Dallas, Texas despite them telling him that he was in Georgia. Tanyah started to tear up as she continued reading and flipping through the pages. Within a day of admission he was experiencing multi-organ failure and his cause of death was a heart attack. She couldn't read anymore and had to put the papers down.

Her shoulders shook as she cried thinking about whether or not he was alert and suffering the whole time. She wondered if he'd asked for her or to speak to her. She wondered whether his family had lied and told him that she'd left him or didn't love him anymore. Did he die not knowing what was going on? Not knowing how much she loved him and had been praying for him to come back. She couldn't continue like this.

Let It Be

The what ifs were too much to handle.

Her mom came over and sat next to her.

"It's too much, mom."

"I know. It's like a tangled ball of yarn and the more you pull and try to untangle it, the more you find out. You're going to make yourself sick if you keep going down this road. I know it's hard. It's not right. If you can let it go, I would let it go. But you know that your dad and I will help you no matter what you decide," she told her.

"Yes, you know that money has never been an issue for us and if you want to fight, then we'll fight. We'll figure it out along the way and you know God always provides," her dad chimed in.

"You're right. I can't do this. I don't want to know anymore, I just want to go home. There's no sense in going broke or into debt trying to fight for someone who isn't even here anymore. They can have whatever they want. I have to let this go or I'm going to go crazy," Tanyah said, now resigned and tired of this horrible game that she'd been made a part of.

It was still early so they decided to hit the road and stop at another RV park once her dad got tired. Tanyah wasn't in any shape to drive so she had to wait until the next day to take over. The ride back wasn't bad and they made it in good time. She decided to just go home with them and hang out until it was time to pick up the twins the day after Christmas.

Most of her Christmas break was spent sleeping or just going through the motions and doing Christmas activities with the rest of her family and her sister's in-laws. She avoided looking out of the windows at her parents' house or glancing across the street when she went outside. The pain of all their memories from childhood when Taurrean lived across the street was

That One Time My Mother-in-Law Kidnapped My Husband

enough to stop her heart.

* * *

Tanyah finally received a copy of the death certificate in January after having to jump through more hoops in order to get it. As she read over the document, she started to see red. She hadn't expected more lies and deceit. It had been a month. She read over the top fields multiple times in disbelief. She didn't even know that someone could lie on a death certificate, and yet they had. Or rather Taurrean's father had reported the lies. She knew that he was complicit in everything that happened, but she had no clue he would also go to these extremes. Something like this was more on Evelyn and Sharee's level.

Taurrean was listed as a resident of Georgia instead of Texas and his parents' mailing address was used. His employment and job status had been made up and it said that he was a package handler who worked for the Postal Service. That piece alone pissed Tanyah off and almost made her rip the whole thing into shreds. How dare he diminish Taurrean's hard work in becoming a supervisor for a huge logistics company that had locations in multiple states? Did he even know anything about him? He'd never worked for the post office. Hell, he didn't even check the damn mail half of the time! Tanyah had a slight smile remembering yelling at him for leaving all of the bills in the mailbox for her to get and just grabbing the coupons he wanted from the junk pages.

The next part broke her heart all over again. Under marital status, his dad put that he was married, but separated and that the spouse was unattainable. They didn't even have the decency to put her name. The same people who'd once treated her as a daughter even when they weren't married, who'd known her since she was ten years old. Tanyah set the paper down on her table and took a deep breath. She'd said that she wasn't going to sue them or pursue any legal action, but now she was furious. If nothing else ever got done, she vowed to get his death certificate corrected, no matter what it took. And she was going to report her damn car stolen even though she didn't really want it back.

As she scanned through the rest of the fields, she froze on the date and time of death. Everything was at a standstill as her eyes blurred in and out of focus. She blinked a few times and it still read the same thing. *Date pronounced dead, 12/09/16. Time pronounced dead, 1:10 am. Cause of death, heart attack.*

Tanyah ran to the bathroom and barely made it as she began to cry and throw up everything she'd eaten earlier that day. She couldn't believe what she was seeing. The implications alone had her shook. Tanyah had woken up that same morning, at the exact same time, and recalled feeling like she was having a heart attack. The pain had subsided and she'd felt like a weight had been lifted from her, but never in a million years would she have thought that she possibly felt him when he died hundreds of miles away. She remembered that she'd written him one of her letters about it and even told her mom later that day and ran to grab her notebook to confirm. She flipped through the pages and, sure enough, the entry was there; yet she still couldn't believe it.

The next few months went by in a blur of basketball games, track meets, and work. Tanyah was like a robot and really couldn't remember anything that happened from day to day. She closed herself off and didn't talk to many people outside of

Porsha, Steff, and Henry. Tanyah went to work most days, but sometimes she just couldn't do it. Every now and then she'd just skip work entirely and hang out watching movies with Henry. Their friendship grew, but she knew it could never be more. She didn't want it to be anything other than that, but she found herself getting attached to him. He was her safe place. It became a regular thing over the summer and since Tommy was still being a great co-parent, she had a lot of time to hang out and do nothing. Things would eventually get back to normal... Or would they?

The End'ish

Epilogue

Tanyah jogged stealthily through the thick wooded area. It was dark, and the moon barely did the huge white oak trees justice. Their wide canopies and massive horizontal limbs provided the perfect cover for anyone who may be out lurking in the dead of night. And on this particular night, it was Tanyah doing the lurking.

She'd been running five times a week under the guise of training for a full marathon the whole year to prepare. Tanyah had scoped out the area and set up camp around thirty miles out just to be on the safe side. Lucky for her, the weather in Georgia was similar to Texas so she didn't have to pack a lot of extra clothing or equipment for the camp site since it wasn't too cold or hot in December.

Tanyah finally reached the small clearing that led to a neighborhood tucked away in a tree-laden area. She moved slowly along the back perimeter, counting the change in fences until she got to the seventh one. Remembering the small hole from before, she crawled through the space and continued towards the looming two-story home staying close to the ground as she approached the back door. Tanyah smirked

That One Time My Mother-in-Law Kidnapped My Husband

at how smart she was. She knew their dog had died. She also knew that they were lazy and wouldn't get rid of the doggy door. Besides, there was hardly any crime in that affluent part of town. The only criminals that she knew of would be asleep inside of the house.

Tanyah slunk through the opening and held the magnetic flap with her tennis shoes so that it wouldn't slam shut once she got through. She slowly stood up and looked around while her eyes adjusted to the darkness. Tanyah crept through the kitchen and turned the corner to look out of the front windows. There was only one car in the driveway, which meant that this would be easy. She smiled and moved slowly up the stairs without making a sound.

At the top of the stairs, Tanyah heard a familiar, annoying snore and gently removed the Glock 19 from her shoulder holster. She pulled out her silencer from the other pocket and put it on the gun. Her hands shook as she held the gun out in front of her and walked carefully towards the master bedroom.

The moonlight slithered through an upstairs window illuminating an old family photo. A young, familiar face smiled back at her causing a tear to fall down her face. She blinked several times and shook her head so that she could concentrate. The room door was already ajar so she didn't have to worry about the jambs creaking like they normally would in the movies.

Tanyah stood at the bottom of the bed. She clicked the safety to the off position and aimed her gun as she waited for the small sound to register in the sleeping woman's brain and wake her up from her obnoxious slumber.

"Tanyah?" came the sleepy reply, followed by a panicked scream, "Tanyah?!"

"Evelyn," Tanyah said quietly, without any emotion as she

Epilogue

pulled the trigger.

Tanyah clutched her chest in agony. Something wasn't right. She looked down and saw blood-stained hands and a pool of blood formed under her shirt.

"What the f-"

Tanyah jumped up and fell from the couch grabbing her chest and breathing hard. She turned over on the hardwood floor and found her phone. It was 1:10 am. Again. She climbed back onto the couch and hit the light switch for the Christmas tree behind her. It had been almost a year since Taurrean died and she was still haunted with nightmares and would wake up every now and then with soul crushing, phantom chest pains. She prayed for relief, but it only came sometimes. So she'd discovered the wonderful world of muscle relaxers. The fact that they were an intoxicating drug that caused an extreme sense of calmness and euphoria, along with almost immediate drowsiness, often meant that she was asleep most of the time.

There still wasn't much movement with the death certificate getting corrected and she didn't even bother to think about it until she got a random email from the lawyers in Georgia. Mr. Breeden finally got the name and address of the cemetery where Taurrean had been buried. Tanyah immediately replied to the email thanking him and his office for continuing to work on getting information for her after a whole year. She dialed the number for the Bridgewood Memorial Cemetery.

"Hello, Bridgewood Memorial Cemetery. How can I help you?"

"Hi. My name is Tanyah Watson. My husband is buried there and I wanted to come see his grave site; but, I've never been to one before, so I just wanted to get some direction on what to do or where to go once I get there. Can you help?"

That One Time My Mother-in-Law Kidnapped My Husband

Tanyah asked.

"Sure, Ms. Watson and I'm sorry for your loss. My name is Walter. Can you give me your husband's name and date of death please?"

"Yes, thank you. He actually died a little over a year ago on December 9, 2016. Taurrean Watson."

"Okay, give me a second to look that up," Walter said kindly and began typing on his keyboard.

"Okay," Tanyah replied.

"Um, ma'am? What did you say your name was again?" he asked as he joined the conversation again.

"Tanyah. Tanyah Watson."

"Okay, let me put you on hold for just a moment."

"Okay," Tanyah said, hesitating a bit.

After a few minutes, Walter came back on the line and told her that there was an issue with his system and that he would have to call her back. When three days passed and she still hadn't heard back and all of her calls were being taken down as messages, she decided that it was time to finally make another trip to Georgia.

When she arrived, she stopped at the police station to check in on her stolen vehicle report. They hadn't contacted her before and she didn't care enough to contact them either; but since she was in town, she figured she should at least ask. Officer Cato was still there and greeted her with a smile. He said that they were still unable to locate her other car in Georgia. It seemed that the family was either hiding it or had gotten rid of it somehow because the car wasn't at any of the addresses for the properties they owned.

Tanyah let him know that she had not heard from Taurrean's family, and even though she tried to reach out to his ex-wife

Epilogue

and kids, she never heard from them either. He apologized for everything that she'd been through and then finally asked her what had brought her to Georgia. She explained the suspicious behavior of the man working for the cemetery and said that all she wanted was to just go see her husband's grave site.

Officer Cato escorted her in his police cruiser about five miles down the road. She didn't realize how close it had been this whole time. It wasn't far from Taurrean's parent's house either. Officer Cato decided to go in and request all of the information on his own. He had a soft spot for Tanyah and didn't want her to go through any more pain on his watch if he could help it.

He returned to the car with a small smile and drove her around to the grave site. It was at the back of the property and a large white oak tree seemingly provided the perfect cover from inclement weather along with a little privacy. He walked over to the headstone with her and quickly paid his respects. He squeezed her hand and told her to take her time as he walked back to his vehicle.

Tanyah didn't have any tears left. She stared at the grave in silence for a few minutes and then put the flowers she'd brought with her into the holder on the side.

"I'm sorry I couldn't save you, sweetheart. I'm sorry that I wasn't here. I've loved you my whole life, and I always will. Until we meet again," she whispered to the dirt and kissed the headstone.

Tanyah thanked Officer Cato again for everything and let him know that she'd be heading out of town early the next morning on a red-eye flight. He gave her a hug and told her to take care of herself. She drove off in the opposite direction of her hotel and came to Evelyn and Rick's neighborhood. She

That One Time My Mother-in-Law Kidnapped My Husband

dropped a note in their mailbox and then left.

I hope you all rot in hell. -Tanyah

Want more? Keep reading to see what happens next in The Tanyah Series with a newly released excerpt from Book #3, That One Time I Kinda Went to Jail.

Chapter 1: New Orleans

October 21, 2018
Sunday

Tanyah had zoned out temporarily as she felt the buzz start to kick in from the amaretto sour she'd downed to take the edge off from watching Henry get fondled by the super-hot stripper on stage. Her eyes flashed red as she watched the girl pull herself up on the pole to do a heel clack and then land on top of Henry's dick in a full-on split.

"Aaaaayyyeeee!!"

Several people from the audience cheered and screamed at the performance. His cousin, Kris, was sitting next to her eyeing Tanyah's reaction and smiling. Tanyah grabbed his drink from him and took the rest of it to the head. He smirked at her.

"You're gonna regret that later," he said as he shook his head and grabbed a lemon pepper wing from the basket.

Tanyah wasn't a drinker at all, but her few trips to see Henry in New Orleans after he'd moved had her building up the courage to drink more. Plus, his family partied each weekend she was there, and they always had daiquiris or something

That One Time My Mother-in-Law Kidnapped My Husband

tasty for her to try alongside the amazing food they cooked.

After hanging out all day eating, visiting with his relatives, and a little sightseeing around town, Henry had dragged Tanyah out with him to the strip club where his best friend was working the DJ booth for the night. His cousin decided to meet them there after being convinced by the promise of some good-ass wings.

Tanyah waved one of the waitresses over and asked for some water before grabbing a wing for herself. She was still stuffed from all of the food she'd been eating that weekend but needed something to control her facial expressions as she watched the stripper dance all over her man.

Well, he wasn't hers at all. Hell, she didn't even want a relationship, but it didn't matter. Something about him being touched by another woman had her jealous juices flowing unreasonably. If she'd been one of those immortal creatures from the books she read, her fangs would have begun to elongate as she prepared to pounce on the poor, unsuspecting girl and rip her throat out.

Luckily, the song ended as Tanyah felt herself stand up. She was drunk as fuck and about to attack this chick like she was a damn vampire. *Get it together, girl. You're definitely trippin'.*

"I'm going to the bathroom real quick. Order me another drink, but not anything too strong," Tanyah said to Henry as he laughed and made his way back to the sitting area they'd been in. She didn't have to go but needed an explanation for standing up after the music had just stopped.

Tanyah checked her face in the bathroom mirror and saw that she was flushed. Her light brown skin had a crimson tint and sweat was starting to bead on her forehead. *Yep, definitely, a little bit gone.*

Chapter 1: New Orleans

She figured she might as well try to use the bathroom since she was already there and entered a stall. It turned out to be a great idea. As soon as she started to squat, she had to release what felt like twenty pounds of instant pressure from her bladder.

After washing her hands and splashing her face a little with some water, she was ready to go back and try to take on the rest of the night. It was already 2 am, and way past her usual 8 pm bedtime. She swayed a bit as she approached the couch and Henry handed her another drink.

Tanyah plopped down onto the sofa next to Kris and smiled as she began munching on another wing. The stripper was standing next to her chatting up Henry and the DJ while he took a break. As it turned out, her name was Krystal, and she was pretty cool. Tanyah loosened up and talked to her about pole dancing techniques, complimenting her on a few tricks she had seen her do when they first walked in.

Tanyah's alter ego was a pole dancer, and she had a personal pole in her room at home. She blushed as she remembered video chatting with Henry while he was at the same strip club a few weeks ago and swinging around her pole to the music playing in the background. She'd also almost fallen asleep in class the next day because they'd been on the phone all night until almost 3 am.

The room was starting to spin and collapse upon itself a little as Tanyah continued sipping her drink. She was so thirsty. And then it hit her. Tanyah was high. She laughed so hard that the rum punch almost came out of her nose. She'd only taken a few puffs before they had entered the club. Kris looked at her and started laughing as well.

"Bruh, what the hell is going on?" he asked as he continued

That One Time My Mother-in-Law Kidnapped My Husband

laughing and shaking his head.

"So, I think the high just kicked in, or I just noticed, and now my face hurts from laughing," Tanyah responded while covering her mouth and trying to get herself back under control.

Henry leaned over and whispered in her ear, "You good?"

His breath tickled her ear, and she briefly closed her eyes. That was all the prompting she needed as her core started to moisten her thong panties. Tanyah looked up and smiled, seductively licking her lips.

"I think I'm ready to go. I have to fuck you. Now," she said with a wink.

Henry raised his eyebrows and smiled back as he shook his head. His eyes glowed against the strobe lighting as he leaned in to tell his homeboy that they were about to leave soon. Once he'd paid the tab and said the rest of his goodbyes, they headed out to the car. Tanyah hugged Kris and threw a lazy wave over her shoulder to everyone else.

The ocean breeze blew through the windows as he drove them back to his mom's house, where they were staying for the night. His furniture hadn't arrived yet for his place, and his mom had several spare bedrooms, so it worked out perfectly. Plus, she had a feeling that they might all still be awake and having fun out on the patio where they'd left them earlier. She secretly hoped they had already gone to bed though.

Parties and clubs were still popping around town with no looks of stopping any time soon. You could hear music blaring in the streets from cars and clubs alike. And where there was music, there was twerking. Lots of it. Even in the parking lots.

Tanyah stole a quick glance at Henry's profile as he leaned back with one hand on the steering wheel. Damn, this man was

Chapter 1: New Orleans

fine. Under any other circumstances, she would have gladly entertained the idea of them being a couple and would have chased him until he gave in.

They just functioned so well as friends, with the occasional subtle flirting. And usually, that was the perfect type of relationship to have. Tanyah didn't want things to change between them, even though she toyed with the idea now and again, but tonight the alcohol had her ready to risk it all.

They pulled up to the house and parked on the side of the road. The carport and back porch lights were left on for them as they walked around to the side entry and quietly entered the house. Tanyah followed Henry through the kitchen and down the thin hallway to the first room. He'd put both of their bags in the room earlier before they'd left. Without even thinking about privacy or the fact that the room door was still open, Tanyah lifted her t-shirt over her head and threw it on the bed next to the bag.

Henry gave her a quick once over before he smirked and then grabbed his bag from the floor. He turned towards the door to leave, and she grabbed his hand.

"Where are you going?" she whispered, searching his face for whatever the hell he thought he was about to do.

"I'm going to the other room," he smirked back.

"You're not leaving me in here by myself." She took his bag back from him and then closed and locked the door.

"Oh, that's how you feel?" he asked with an arched eyebrow.

"Don't make me talk anymore before I lose my nerve."

Tanyah flipped the light switch and quickly blinked her eyes to adjust to the soft moonlight peeking through the sheer curtains that were strung loosely across the window. Switching places with him and gently edging him towards the

That One Time My Mother-in-Law Kidnapped My Husband

bed, she slowly pulled Henry's shirt up and off of his body. He wrapped his arms around her and put his hands in her back pockets pulling her towards him and grinding his growing erection into her heated mound.

Her breath caught in her throat as she tried to stifle the moan that was about to come out of her mouth. She bit down on his shoulder and pushed him onto the bed as she shimmied out of her jean shorts and then impatiently undid his belt buckle and stripped off his cargo shorts to release the steel rod threatening to burst through his zipper.

With one hand, he pulled her on top of him and then palmed her left breast through the lacy bra material. He put his mouth over the fabric wetting her hardened nipple and slowly dragging his tongue over the tight bud before lightly nipping it with his teeth. Tanyah pulled her bra down to grant him access as he stealthily moved her thong to the side and slipped one of his fingers inside of her.

"Fuckin' hell…" Tanyah whispered as her eyes rolled to the back of her head while she tried to contain her pleasure.

"Mmm hmm," Henry hummed around her nipple before switching to the other and putting half her breast in his mouth. He pressed his thumb to her clit as he slowly moved his finger in and out of her center.

He was going to drive her crazy and make her wake up the whole damn house, so she pulled back to give herself a little break and removed her bra and panties. She lowered her body to straddle his legs and took him into her mouth. She felt him twitch and smiled around him as she stroked his length up and down with her hand and swirled her tongue around the head. He slid his fingers over her wet folds and then gripped her hip as she found his spot.

Chapter 1: New Orleans

"This is going to be over real quick if you keep doing that," Henry mumbled, his voice now husky and deeper than normal.

Tanyah moved up his body, kissing and licking every inch of him as she positioned her dripping core over his dick. She was so wet he slid right in without any assistance, and they both stopped breathing. Henry shut his eyes, and Tanyah stilled her body as she felt herself ripple and flutter around his thick member.

"Fuck," he whispered.

Tanyah waited a few more moments and then began to grind and swivel her hips slowly on his dick. He let her have control until he couldn't take it anymore and then let out a low growl as he grabbed her hips and started bouncing her up and down, her ass making soft clapping sounds against his thighs. She let her head fall back as she rubbed her bundle of nerves in a frantic circular motion while she came undone beneath him.

Henry pumped into her hard from the bottom a few times and then pulled her down to him as he exploded inside of her and kissed her deeply to stifle both of their moans. Tanyah licked and sucked his bottom lip before gently biting him and rolling over to her side.

"God, I hope I'm not too drunk, and I still remember this in the morning," she said breathlessly.

Henry muffled his laugh and just shook his head.

October 22, 2018
Monday

Tanyah woke up and showered early so that she could get back on the road. Of course, Henry had already been awake and gone through his whole routine. He was a huge morning person. She wanted to stay longer and go out for breakfast, but she had to be in court over some foolishness with her ex-

That One Time My Mother-in-Law Kidnapped My Husband

husband, Tommie, the next day, so she chose to hurry up and get back to Texas. Interestingly enough, she was wide awake and felt well-rested for the long drive ahead, despite the wild weekend.

She thanked the universe that she didn't have a hangover and smiled at herself in the mirror after brushing her teeth. Henry's mom had headed out to work already, and she made sure to pop her head out into the hallway to thank her for the hospitality and say goodbye. She overheard her asking Henry what time they'd gotten in last night and then saying that she'd only gone in about an hour before they got back and laughing about one of his aunts being drunk.

Once Tanyah finished packing up her bag, she met Henry in the kitchen so that he could walk her outside. Always the gentleman, he took her bag and held the door open for her as she stepped out and headed toward her car.

She opened up the passenger door for him to put the bag inside. He walked with her around to the driver's side and then leaned up against the back of his car while she played with her car keys nervously in her hands.

"You took advantage of me last night," Henry said in an accusing voice.

That cut the tension in the air as Tanyah doubled over and laughed.

"And in my mom's house!" he pretended to be appalled.

"Whatever, I was drunk," Tanyah said as she playfully punched his arm. "Besides, you liked it," she added with a smirk and a slow glance toward his crotch.

"I'm not a piece of meat," he said as he turned his nose up in the air.

"Yes, you are. Now, give me a hug so I can get on this road,"

Tanyah chuckled.

They embraced as friends like nothing had even happened the night before, and she stepped back a little, looking into his eyes.

"Can I kiss you goodbye?" Tanyah asked shyly.

He returned her intense gaze and leaned toward her. She took that as a yes and kissed him gently on his lips before grinning and pulling herself away.

"Aight, homie. I'm gone," she said as she hopped into her car and chunked him the deuce.

"I'll check on you periodically until you get home. Me and Nole are going to get barbecue again later," he responded with a smile, knowing she was going to be jealous and sad about missing out on the delicious food.

"Ugh, just rub it in, why don't you!"

It wasn't too late when Tanyah returned home from New Orleans since it had only taken her around eight and a half hours. But she was tired. She called Henry while she unpacked her stuff to let him know that she made it and promised to call him in the morning before court…

About the Author

J. Washington is an urban fiction author who writes stories that combine comedic tragedy, dysfunctional families, and unbelievable plots. She enjoys relaxing at home, tinkering with technology, being a part-time actress, and experimenting with different cake-decorating projects. She's an avid reader, loves working out, and is pretty much a total nerd in disguise! This new chapter of becoming an author has been one of her favorite aliases yet.

You can connect with me on:
- http://www.dopekontent.com/j-washington-author
- https://www.facebook.com/JWashingtonAuthor
- https://www.amazon.com/author/washingtonj
- https://www.goodreads.com/jwashingtonauthor

Also by J. Washington

Check out the other titles in The Tanyah Series. Book #1 will be coming at a later date!!!

That One Time I Kinda Went to Jail
Book #3 in The Tanyah Series

Made in the USA
Middletown, DE
08 March 2023